GROSS ANATOMY

By Christine Becker, R.N., B.S.N.
Illustrated by Mary Bryson, M.A.M.S.

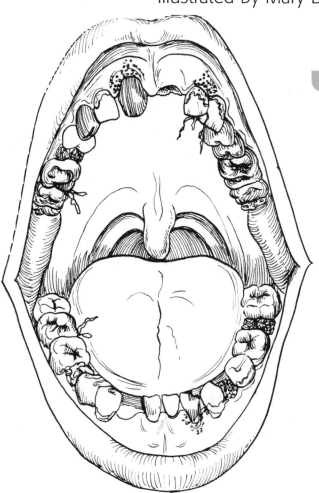

Random House **NEW YORK**

To my father and stepmother, Cliff and Mary Becker, for giving me the dream of writing, and to my boyfriend, Walter James, for making that dream a reality.—C.B.

To my husband, Jamie, my soulmate and the love of my life, to my daughter, Frances, my sparkling inspiration, and to Beth, Gigi, Jan, and John for their good humor.—M.B.

Acknowledgments:
Special thanks to Charlene Hyde, Ph.D., and to those at UCLA who allowed me to "pick their brains": Dr. Warwick Peacock, Dr. Bernard Churchill, Dr. Richard Ehrlich, Dale Perry, R.N., M.S., and especially Laurie Reyen, R.N., M.S.

ISBN: 0-679-88187-5

Library of Congress Catalog Card Number: 96-67832

Printed in the United States of America

10 9 8 7 6 5 4 3 2 1

Contents

the INTEGUMENTARY SYSTEM

The *integument* (in-TEG-yuh-ment), or skin, is the largest organ of the human body. As an outer covering, the integument guards the body and all of its internal organs against infection or sudden injury. Without this protective barrier, our bodies would be instantly attacked by invading bacteria, fungi, parasites, and viruses.

     The skin also plays a role in helping to regulate the body's temperature. Tiny *sudoriferous* (soo-duh-RIFF-er-us)—or sweat-bearing—glands in the skin pour perspiration onto the surface of our bodies. As the sweat evaporates into the air, it cools the skin, keeping us from overheating in normal circumstances.

     These functions of the skin are essential to life. If we had no integument, we would quickly die from infection or bleeding.

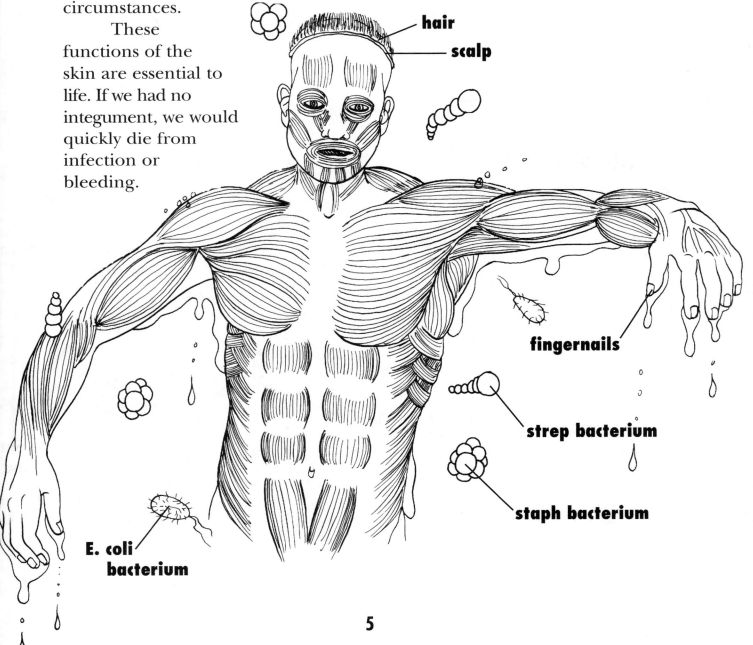

hair

scalp

fingernails

strep bacterium

staph bacterium

E. coli bacterium

SKIN

From pasty white to brownish black, human skin comes in a variety of colors. At times, it may even change shades. Emotions, activities, and illness play a role in your hue: exposure to the sun can turn the skin red or brown, fright may turn it white, disease may turn it yellow, and lack of oxygen can even turn it blue.

In addition to temporarily changing color, the skin undergoes numerous transformations throughout our lives. It grows in size from our infancy to our adulthood, heals when cut (under most conditions), stretches with weight gain, and becomes wrinkled with the passage of time.

The skin consists of three layers. The top layer, or *epidermis*, is made up of flattened, dehydrated cells that are constantly shed. Beneath the epidermis lies the *dermis*. It contains blood vessels, hair follicles, and nerves. The deepest layer of tissue, or *hypodermis*, consists mostly of fat cells—even in thin people! The fat provides cushioning and warmth to the internal organs.

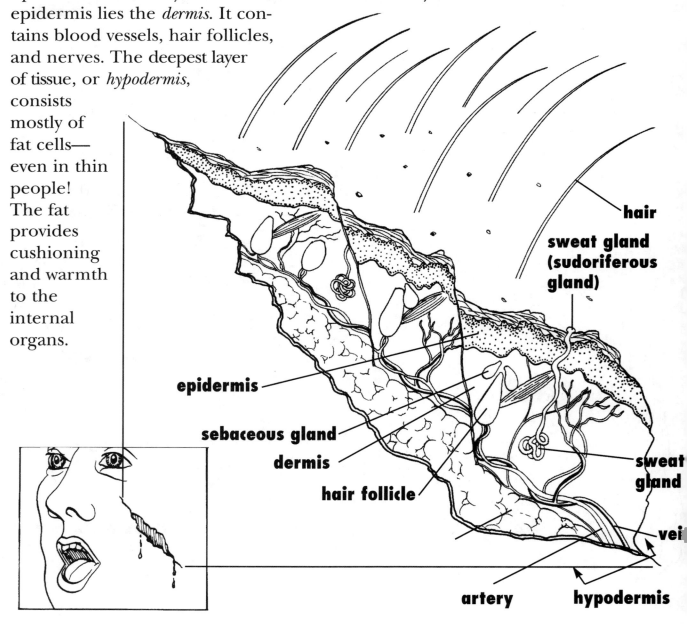

hair

sweat gland (sudoriferous gland)

epidermis

sebaceous gland

dermis

hair follicle

sweat gland

vei[n]

artery

hypodermis

COMMON SKIN CONDITIONS

Thousands of skin conditions exist, but here are some of the more common ones, called *lesions* (LEE-zhuns). If you have not already found these flaws on your flesh, you probably will in the future.

BRUISE: After an injury, such as a fall or punch in the face, a bluish purple mark called a bruise may appear on your skin. Bruises occur when blood vessels are injured, causing blood to leak into surrounding tissue. As this leaked blood is resorbed (absorbed again) by the body, healing bruises lighten in color to brown, then greenish yellow, before disappearing completely.

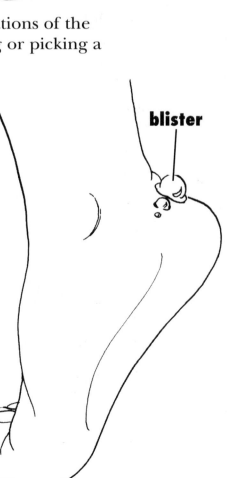

bruise

WART: These firm, roughened bumps caused by a virus (and not, as rumored, by toads) are examples of *papules* (PAP-yoolz), small, solid, and raised inflammations of the skin. Touching or picking a wart can cause it to spread. Doctors may remove warts by either freezing or burning them off the body.

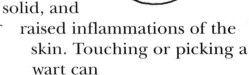

wart

blister

BLISTER: Usually caused by a burn or continuous friction (like a tight shoe rubbing the heel), a blister is technically known as a *vesicle* (VES-ih-kull), a lesion that appears as a fluid-filled little bump. Blisters are filled with clear, sticky fluid that eventually dries up on its own. Do not pop a blister, or you may find yourself with a gooey, infected sore.

PIMPLE: An oil gland swollen with bacteria-laden pus, a pimple is an example of a skin irregularity named a *pustule* (PUS-chule). A pustular lesion is an elevated area of skin that is filled with pus-like, or *purulent* (PURE-yuh-lent), matter.

SCAB: A mixture of dried pus and blood, a scab is a crust that covers and protects a wound as it heals.

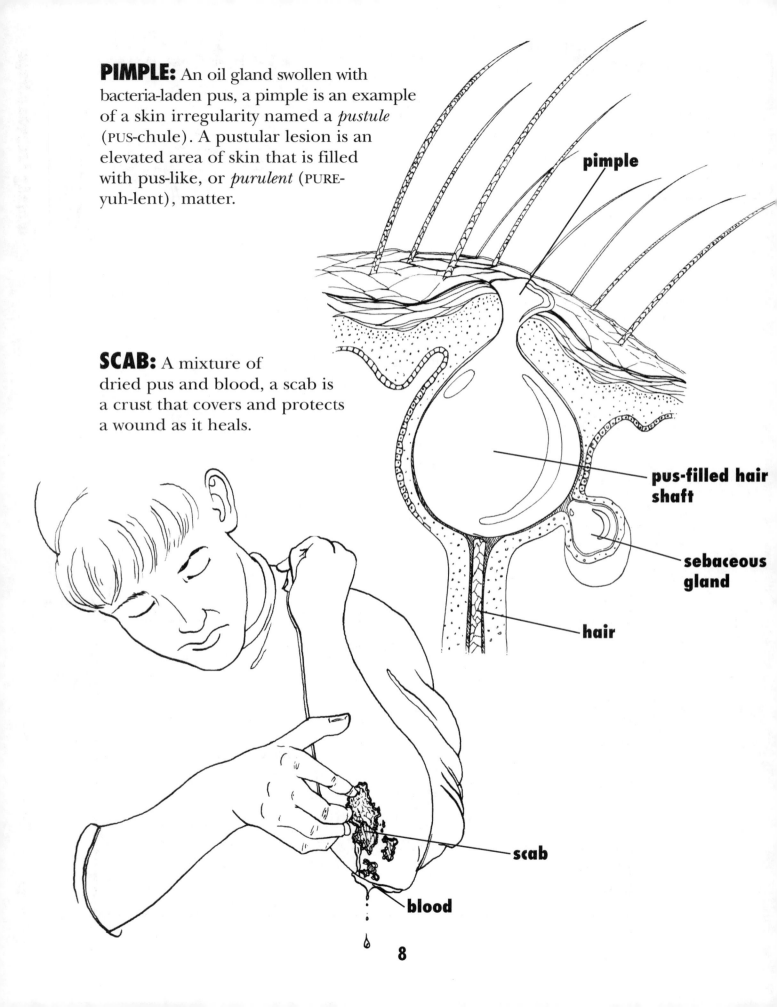

pimple

pus-filled hair shaft

sebaceous gland

hair

scab

blood

ATHLETE'S FOOT: A skin infection caused by a fungus that creeps between the toes, under the nails, and onto the soles of the feet. Warm, sweaty sneakers are the perfect breeding ground for this foul fungus. As athlete's foot develops, its telltale symptoms—burning, itching blisters and *fissures* (cracks)—appear on the feet. If not properly treated with antifungal creams, athlete's foot can last for years.

athlete's foot

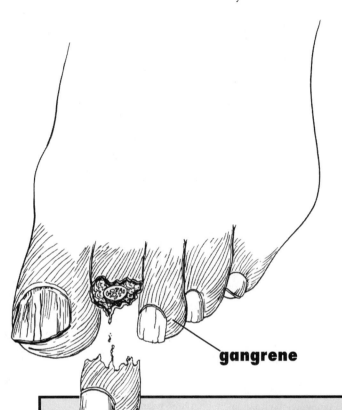

gangrene

GRUESOME GANGRENE

If a traumatic injury or disease, such as diabetes, cuts off the blood supply to a part of the body, the tissue there will begin to die. *Gangrene* (GANG-green), the medical term for this life-threatening disorder, occurs mostly in two forms: dry and wet gangrene.

Dry gangrene mainly strikes the extremities, where the flesh on an affected part (such as a toe) shrivels up, turns black, and eventually falls off. Wet gangrene, which may also affect internal organs, occurs as bacteria infest the dying tissue. The blackened, gangrenous skin becomes moist, swollen, and cold. Bacteria begin to liquefy the body part, releasing a putrid odor. Unless treated, wet gangrene can cause death within a few days.

FOOT AFFLICTIONS

The feet are home to numerous annoying afflictions. *Corns, bunions,* and *jam* may sound like grocery items, but they are not available in any market.

CORNS: These are horny knobs of skin that form over bony areas when constant friction or pressure is applied to the foot. Corns are sometimes surgically shaved or burned off with chemicals by a foot doctor, called a *podiatrist* (puh-DIE-uh-trist).

corn

BUNIONS: Pressure against the foot may also cause *bunions,* which are abnormally enlarged joints at the bases of the big toes. Constant pressure and irritation cause swelling of the *bursa,* a cushiony sac located between the tendon and first bone of the big toe. A swollen bursa causes the big toe to become disfigured, sore, and painful. Surgery may be needed to remove the bursa and realign the crooked big toe.

bunie

TOE JAM: Lint that builds up between the toes is commonly known as *toe jam.* This condition does not require medical treatment—only careful removal of the jam by the afflicted individual. Proper cleaning between the toes serves as prevention for this condition.

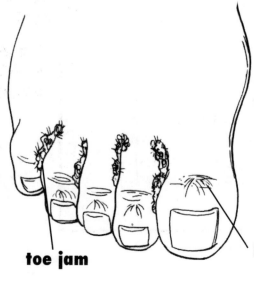

toe jam

hairy toe

10

SCALP

The skin covering the top and back of the head is called the scalp. Whether it is balding or covered with hair, the scalp is home to more than a few offensive afflictions.

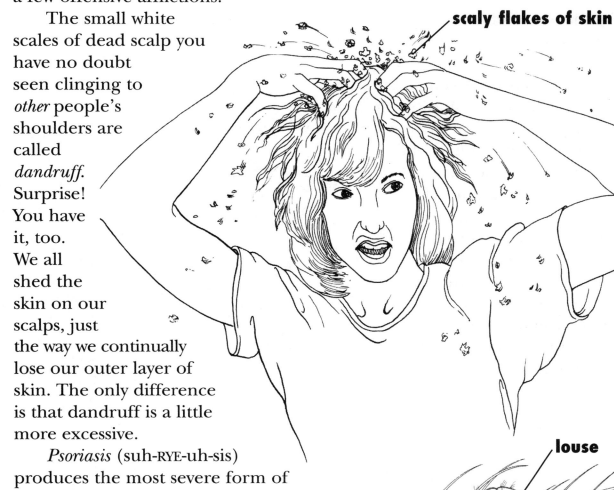

scaly flakes of skin

louse

nit (louse egg)

louse sucking blood

The small white scales of dead scalp you have no doubt seen clinging to *other* people's shoulders are called *dandruff.* Surprise! You have it, too. We all shed the skin on our scalps, just the way we continually lose our outer layer of skin. The only difference is that dandruff is a little more excessive.

Psoriasis (suh-RYE-uh-sis) produces the most severe form of scaling. Here, the scalp goes insane producing epidermal cells, causing red patches cloaked with thick, silvery scales of dead cells to form on the scalp and other body parts.

SCALP SUCKERS

An itching scalp *may* be a signal that something other than dead cells are accumulating on your head. You may have lice! Lice are tiny, wingless insects that cling to the hair shafts and suck blood from a person's scalp. These parasites are easily passed from person to person by sharing combs, brushes, hats, or pillows.

HAIR

When you hear the word "hair," you usually think of the stuff that grows out of your head. Head hair, or *terminal hair,* as it is called, goes through cycles of growth, transition, and rest. This means that every strand of hair on your head will fall out and be replaced in the next two to six years.

Besides your terminal hair, soft, fine *vellus hair* can be found on almost every part of your body except your lips, the palms of your hands, and the soles of your feet. Take a look.

While a head full of hair is usually attractive, a bush of hair protruding from a nostril, ear, or armpit is, in many cultures, not. An extremely hairy back may evoke images of an ape.

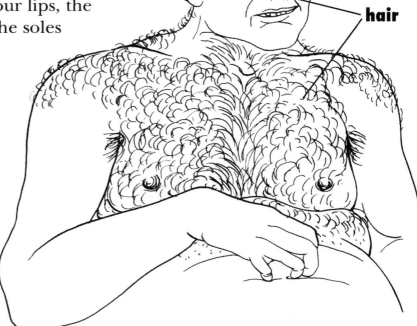

hair

hair

boil

bursting boil

FOUL FOLLICULAR FACTS

When a *bacterium* (back-TIER-ee-um), a microscopic one-celled organism, enters a hair follicle on your body, an infection may develop. These painful, pus-filled, reddened bumps—or boils—can appear anywhere on the surface of the skin. In the center of a boil, skin tissue rots and collects into a core of dead tissues.

Boils, which are a kind of superpimple, should not be squeezed! Squeezing can cause the infection to spread. The dead core of a boil must be allowed to burst and splatter its contents or be resorbed by the body. In severe cases, a doctor may lance the boil with a scalpel, allowing it to drain.

FINGERNAILS AND TOENAILS

Nails are layers of flat, dead cells that cover the tips of fingers and toes. They are made up of the protein keratin. Nails are firmly attached to the fingers and toes by cuticles—strips of hardened skin at the base of each nail.

Nailbiters, take note: You are probably chowing down on more than you think. The area beneath the tip of the nail is a virtual Valhalla for the dirt, germs, nasal mucus, and who knows what else your hands come into contact with.

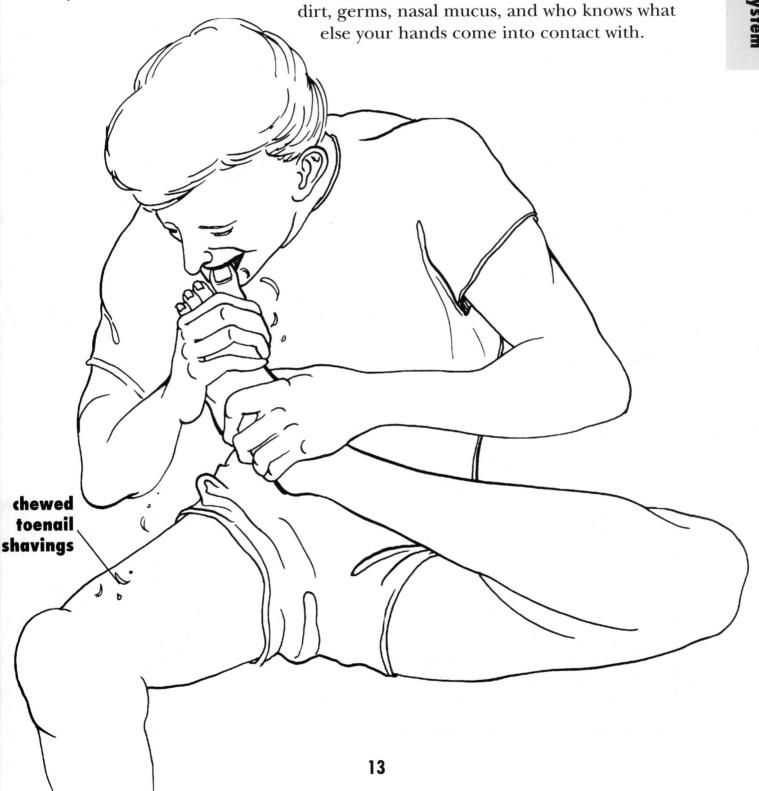

chewed toenail shavings

SUDORIFEROUS GLANDS

Also known as sweat glands, there are two to three million of these tiny perspiration producers located throughout your integument. Most *sudoriferous* (soo-duh-RIFF-er-us) *glands* are *eccrine* (ECK-rin) *glands*, which can be found in great numbers on the forehead, the palms of the hands, and the soles of the feet. The eccrine glands excrete salt, water, and body waste products through the pores and onto your skin in the form of sweat.

apocrine glands

Sweat helps to cool the body when its temperature begins to rise. Although the eccrine glands of an adult produce, on average, 22 ounces of sweat daily, intense heat or vigorous exercise can cause them to produce as much as *95 ounces* in one hour.

The other type of sudoriferous glands, called *apocrine* (AP-uh-krin) *glands,* exist in the armpits, groin, and anal areas. Because they secrete the thicker, slippery fluid that results in body odor, aprocrine glands are also known as *odoriferous* (oh-duh-RIFF-er-us) *glands.*

swea

FOUL FACT

Contrary to popular belief, sweat alone does not cause body odor. In fact, when sweat first reaches the skin's surface, it is entirely odorless. After it is exposed to the air, bacteria break down the waste products contained in the perspiration. The feasting bacteria produce their own waste materials, which are what create body odor.

The MUSCULOSKELETAL SYSTEM

The *musculoskeletal* (MUS-kyuh-loe-SKELL-ih-tul) *system* provides shape, support, mobility, and protection for our bodies. Its main components—bones, cartilage, muscles, and joints—make up more than 70 percent of the human body. Without a musculoskeletal system, our bodies would be piles of quivering flesh and organs. We would not be able to walk or stand or even crawl. If stepped on, we would be easily squashed and most likely instantly killed.

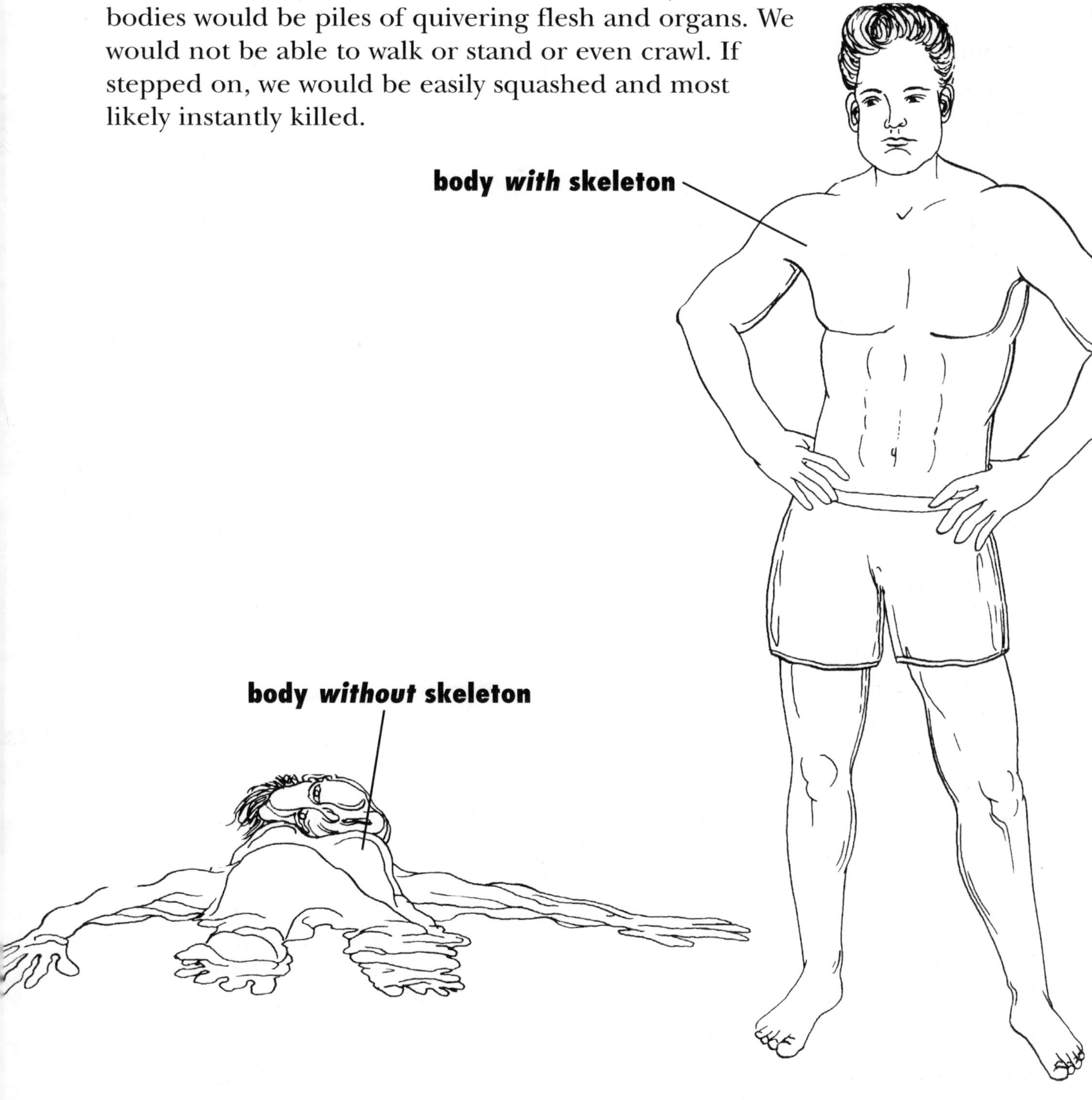

body *with* skeleton

body *without* skeleton

SKELETON

Composed of 206 bones, the skeleton provides a framework for the human body. Fragile organs, such as the heart, lungs, spinal cord, and brain, are encased and protected within the solid skeletal structure.

The four major types of bones include short bones, long bones, flat bones, and irregular bones. Ligaments, bands of connective tissue, hold the bones together.

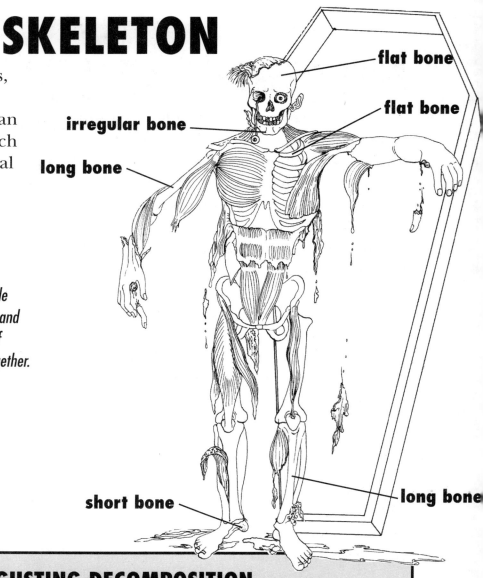

flat bone

flat bone

irregular bone

long bone

short bone

long bone

DISGUSTING DECOMPOSITION

When a person dies and is allowed to rot naturally (i.e., is not preserved or embalmed), bacteria inside the body immediately begin to eat the surrounding flesh. Decomposing blood cells and body gases turn the trunk and thighs green within three days, giving off an awful stench, like that of rotting beef.

The tongue and eyes bulge out, and bloody fluids ooze from the nose, ears, and mouth. The body swells well beyond its once-normal size, and the intestines often fall out of the anus. After about a week, the skin (which has gone from greenish purple to black) falls off the body.

Several weeks after death, the teeth and nails loosen, and the liquefied innards burst. Long after the skin and nails wither away, the bony material of the skeleton remains intact. With time, however, even the solid skeleton will disintegrate, leaving a pile of dust in its place.

SKULL

The skull consists of the fourteen facial bones and the eight bones that form the *cranium*—the brain's protective "helmet." At the time of your birth (if you were delivered vaginally), the bones in your skull squeezed together so that you could pass through your mother's birth canal. The bones may have even overlapped, giving you a coneheaded look.

So how could your skull move without squishing, puncturing, or somehow damaging your brain? Believe it or not, as an infant you had holes and spaces in your head. The holes, called *fontanels* (fon-tun-ELZ), were covered by tough membranes that kept your brain from leaking out. The connective tissue in the spaces between the bones, known as *sutures*, and the fontanels allowed for movement and reshaping of the cranium.

The back, or posterior, fontanel closes by two months of life, and the front, or anterior, fontanel closes within two years. Sutures disappear by age twelve, and the cranial bones interlock.

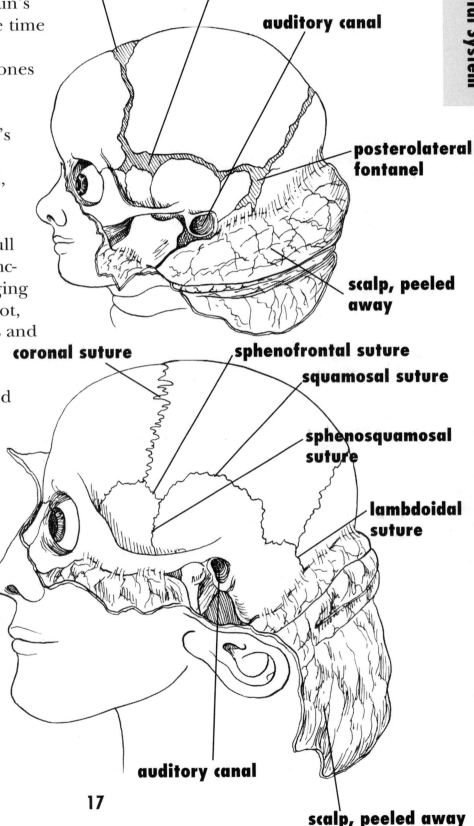

anterior fontanel

anterolateral fontanel

auditory canal

posterolateral fontanel

scalp, peeled away

coronal suture

sphenofrontal suture

squamosal suture

sphenosquamosal suture

lambdoidal suture

auditory canal

scalp, peeled away

BONES

Besides the support and protection they provide to the body, your bones have functions that take place inside of them. Bones act as factories that produce blood cells that will later stream through your arteries and veins. They also serve as storage trunks for important minerals like calcium.

Calcium, phosphorus, and vitamin D are especially important to bone development during infancy and childhood. A diet lacking these elements may lead to a condition of abnormal bone development called rickets. A child suffering rickets has soft, flexible bones and may develop bowlegs or knock-knees, a curved spine, chest deformities like bulging ribs, and an enlarged head.

Poor nutrition can lead to rickets, which can cause skeletal deformities.

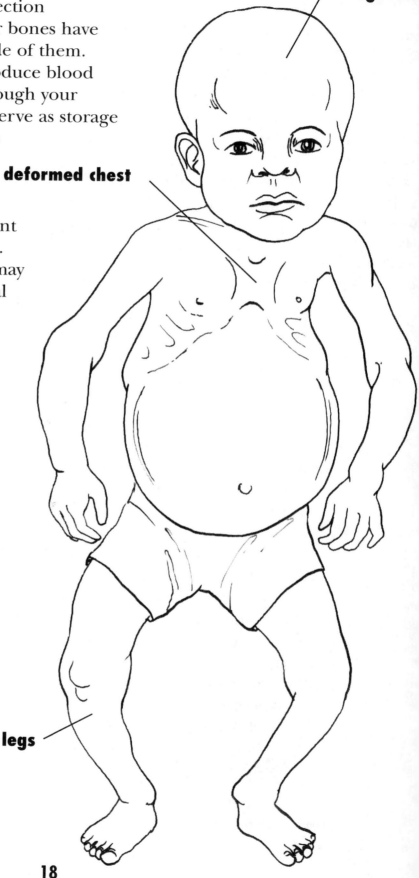

enlarged sk

deformed chest

bowed legs

FRACTURES

Bones change throughout a person's lifetime. During childhood, the skeleton is more fragile because it is made up mostly of cartilage and bone tissues. As a person gets older, the cartilage *ossifies,* or hardens into bone. This means that a young adult's bones are stronger than a child's bones. Bone cells are continually being replaced, keeping bones strong and healthy until a person is between 35 and 40 years old. After that time, bone construction slows down, but bone destruction continues at the same pace. Bone minerals are then lost, making the skeleton brittle and thin.

The soft bones of children and the frail bones of the elderly can easily become *fractured,* or broken. Fractures can be either open or closed. When a *closed* fracture occurs, the skin over the broken bone remains intact. If the fracture is *open,* part of the broken bone is sticking through the skin. A fracture may range in severity from a small hairline crack to the complete shattering of a bone.

greenstick fracture, a crack that does not run completely across the bone

comminuted (kom-uh-NEW-tid) fracture, when the bone is broken into three or more fragments

spiral fracture, caused when a bone breaks as a body part is being twisted

transverse break, which runs straight across the bone

oblique fracture, which slants across the bone

19

MUSCLES

Covering the skeleton are *muscles,* tissues made of fibers that are able to *contract* (tighten) and relax.

The long *striated* (stry-AY-tid) *muscles* are those muscles you have control over. They pull your bones into action, allowing you to run, squat, jump, and smile whenever you want to.

Other types of muscles, known as *smooth muscles,* work *involuntarily* —that is, without your control. An example of smooth muscles at work is your squishing and churning stomach.

Finally, the muscles that make up the heart fall into their own group, called *cardiac muscles.* Cardiac muscles seem to be a combination of the other two types: although they *look* like striated muscles, they *act* involuntarily, like smooth muscles.

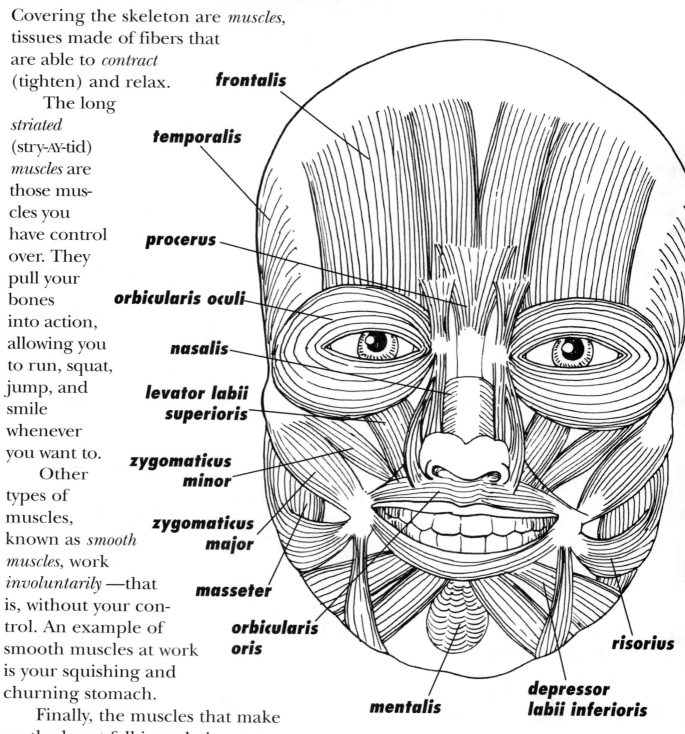

frontalis

temporalis

procerus

orbicularis oculi

nasalis

levator labii superioris

zygomaticus minor

zygomaticus major

masseter

orbicularis oris

mentalis

risorius

depressor labii inferioris

the NERVOUS SYSTEM

The *nervous system* is the communications network for the human body. Bundles of special cells, called *nerves,* allow us to feel sensations like heat, cold, and pain.

When a nerve is triggered by a sensation, it sends off a message in the form of an electrical wave called a *nerve impulse.* This impulse travels to the spinal cord and then up to the brain. Without your brain to make sense of the impulse, you would not recognize that a dead body is foul-smelling or that it hurts to sit on a tack.

Because they are in the center of the network, the brain and the spinal cord are called the *central nervous system.* The smaller nerves that branch to the outer body parts, or the *periphery* of the body, make up the *peripheral nervous system.*

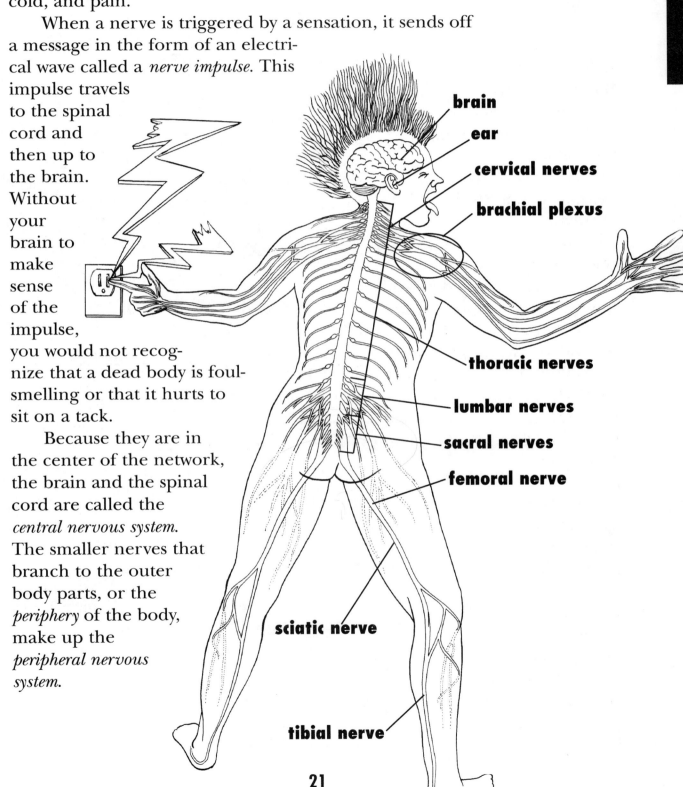

brain

ear

cervical nerves

brachial plexus

thoracic nerves

lumbar nerves

sacral nerves

femoral nerve

sciatic nerve

tibial nerve

BRAIN

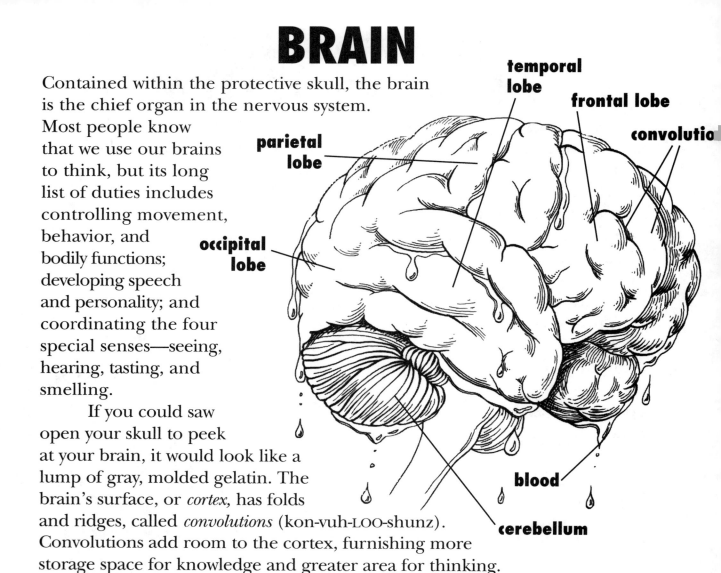

temporal lobe

frontal lobe

convolutio

parietal lobe

occipital lobe

blood

cerebellum

Contained within the protective skull, the brain is the chief organ in the nervous system.

Most people know that we use our brains to think, but its long list of duties includes controlling movement, behavior, and bodily functions; developing speech and personality; and coordinating the four special senses—seeing, hearing, tasting, and smelling.

If you could saw open your skull to peek at your brain, it would look like a lump of gray, molded gelatin. The brain's surface, or *cortex*, has folds and ridges, called *convolutions* (kon-vuh-LOO-shunz). Convolutions add room to the cortex, furnishing more storage space for knowledge and greater area for thinking.

THE BRAIN THAT WOULDN'T DIE

As a work crew blew up rocks at a railroad site in 1848, a 3½'-long pointed iron rod accidentally blasted out of a hole and into the head of the crew's foreman, Phineas Gage.

The impact threw Phineas into the air. He landed in a fit of uncontrollable jerking motion. The rod had struck below his left eye, ripped through his brain, and torn off the front part of his skull.

Then, as blood and brain matter oozed out of the hole in his skull, Phineas sat up and began talking to his shocked crewmen as if nothing had happened.

Thoroughly astounded doctors treated the chatty Phineas, who went on to survive another 12½ years.

bone chunk

brain chunk

bone chunk

blood

SPINAL CORD

Stretching from the brain into the lower back, the *spinal cord* resembles a long white worm covered with blood vessels. Much like the trunk of a tree, the spinal cord branches off into thousands of miles of tiny nerves that reach all parts of the body. When the nerves send out their impulses, these electrical waves travel first to the spinal cord, then up into the brain. This all happens in less than a second.

Because it is such an integral part of the nervous system, the spinal cord is protectively encased within the bony backbone. An injury to the spinal cord cuts off the communication of impulses between the nerve branches and the brain. This can cause *paralysis* (puh-RAL-uh-sis), which is the loss of feeling and movement in parts of the body.

If the damage occurs to the lower part of the cord, only the lower impulses are blocked, paralyzing the body below the waist. When the damage takes place on the higher part of the cord, it blocks off all nerve impulses from below the neck. In this case, the entire body, except the head and neck, will suffer paralysis.

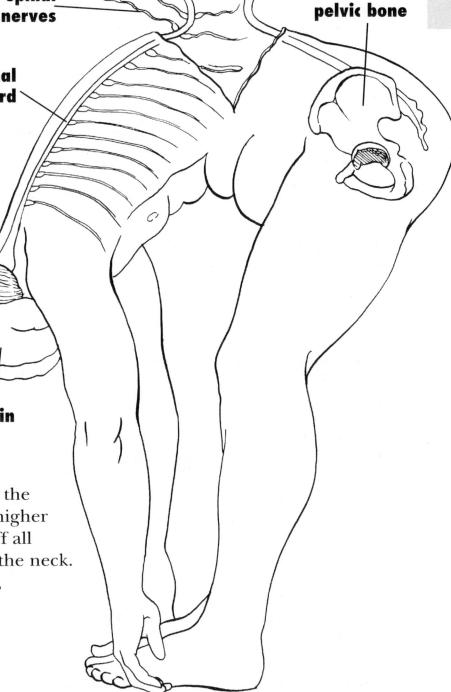

spinal nerves

pelvic bone

spinal cord

brain

SENSORY ORGAN: THE EYES

Our eyes take in visual images of the environment in much the same way that a camera snaps a picture. The *optic*, or eye, nerve sends these images to the brain in the form of nerve impulses. The brain then interprets the images, and what you see in your head is like developed photos.

If you were to pluck an eye from its socket, you might be surprised how much it feels like a big grape. And like a grape, if you drop one and step on it, an eyeball will pop and splatter its contents.

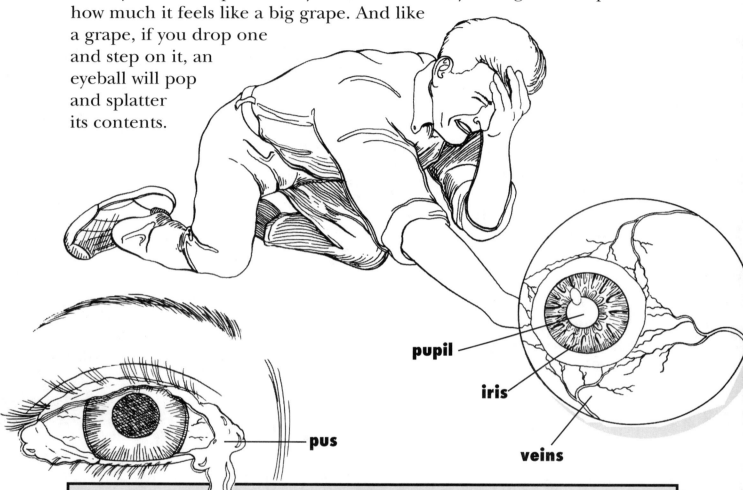

pupil

iris

veins

pus

CRUSTY CONJUNCTIVITIS

Have you ever woken up to find your eyes glued shut with crust? As you pried the lids apart, did you find your eyeballs were swollen and red? As the day moved on, did gobs of pus obscure your vision?

If so, you may have been suffering from *conjunctivitis* (con-junk-tuh-VIE-tis), or pinkeye. Pinkeye is caused by a bacterial or viral infection in the eye.

Highly contagious, pinkeye is spread when infectious material from a crusty eye is rubbed into a clear eye by a soiled tissue or dirty hand.

SENSORY ORGAN: THE EARS

The ear picks up sound waves that are sent through the ear canal to the inner ear. There, the waves are changed to nerve impulses and sent to the brain.

When scratching inside the ear, you may pull out a fingernail full of gooey brown wax. This earwax, called *cerumen* (suh-ROO-mun), is secreted by a type of sweat gland located in the external ear canal.

Cerumen, in moderate amounts, is helpful to the ear. It traps dirt, preventing it from entering the ear. Because earwax is acidic, it also kills bacteria. Its moisture prevents the very sensitive skin of the ear canal from drying out.

If the earwax becomes excessive and packed too tightly, hearing may become difficult. Doctors sometimes prescribe ear drops to loosen the wax, so that a special cerumen spoon can be used to scoop it out.

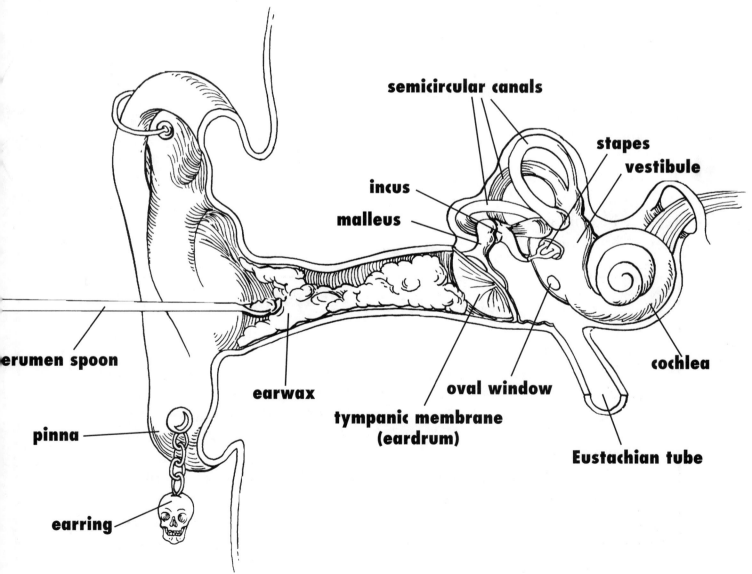

semicircular canals

stapes

vestibule

incus

malleus

cerumen spoon

cochlea

earwax

oval window

pinna

tympanic membrane
(eardrum)

Eustachian tube

earring

SENSORY ORGAN: THE NOSE

The *olfactory* (ohl-FACK-tuh-ree) *organs,* located in the roof of the nasal cavity, detect scents. As we inhale normally, bits of aroma filter through the nostrils and are trapped in mucus produced by the olfactory organs. Sniffing sucks air higher into the nose, trapping even more of the aroma.

Sensory hairs protruding from the olfactory organs detect the aroma and send a nerve impulse to the *olfactory bulb.* This bulb delivers the information straight to the brain, which then identifies the odor.

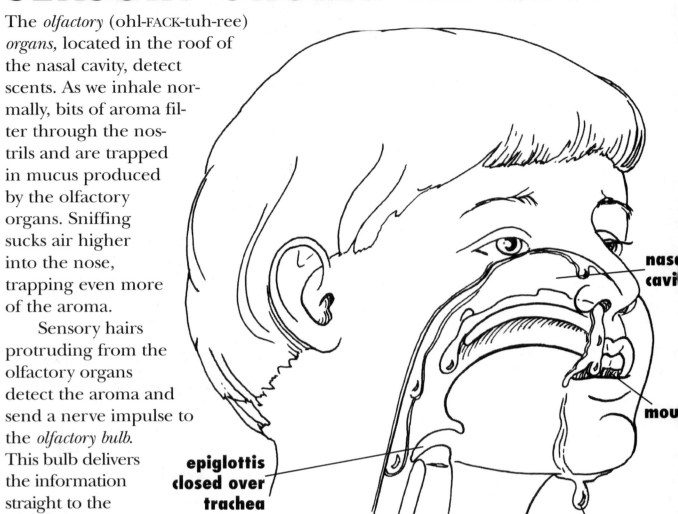

nas[e]
cavi[ty]

mou[th]

epiglottis closed over trachea

esophagus

blood

NAUSEATING NOSEBLEEDS

Nosebleeds can be caused by an irritation of the mucous membrane, like that caused by allergies, violent sneezing, infection, or trauma. The most common cause of nosebleeds, however, is nosepicking.

In the past, people were taught to tilt their heads backward if their noses started bleeding. But leaning the head backward makes blood run into the stomach, sometimes causing nausea. Doctors currently recommend tilting the head forward and pinching the nostrils to halt a nosebleed. In addition, applying ice to the nose may stop the bleeding even faster.

SENSORY ORGAN: THE TONGUE

The taste buds on the tongue possess the ability to distinguish tastes. While they would likely be tickled by the taste of pizza, your taste buds would certainly cause you to spit out a glass of sour milk.

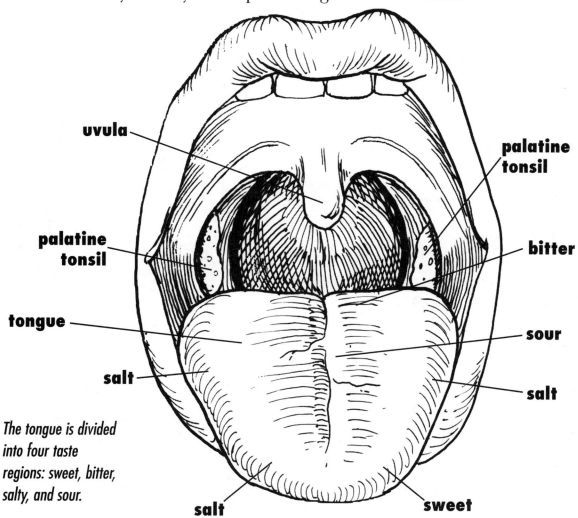

uvula

palatine tonsil

palatine tonsil

bitter

tongue

salt

sour

salt

The tongue is divided into four taste regions: sweet, bitter, salty, and sour.

salt

sweet

CREEPY CRAVINGS

Have you ever yearned for a lunch of cigarette butts and paint chips? *Pica* (PIE-kuh), an appetite disorder, is the craving for non-food substances. The word "pica" comes from the Latin word for magpie, a bird known for its enormous and less-than-choosy diet.

Nutritional deficiencies, mental illness, and pregnancy can cause a person to crave such bizarre breakfasts as pencils, dirt, glue, clay, crayons, matches, or even hair!

the ENDOCRINE SYSTEM

The *endocrine system* is made up of a group of glands that give off chemical messengers called *hormones*. These hormones circulate in the bloodstream and give instructions to the body and the brain. Hormones tell your body when to grow taller and when to grow hair in your armpits, among other things.

One hormone—the antidiuretic hormone, or "ADH"—even gives your body specific instructions concerning the amount it should urinate! Vomiting, diarrhea, and intense exercise, for example, sap your body of needed fluids. To prevent *dehydration,* or the excessive loss of body fluids, ADH tells the body to lay off urine production, retaining more fluid in your blood vessels.

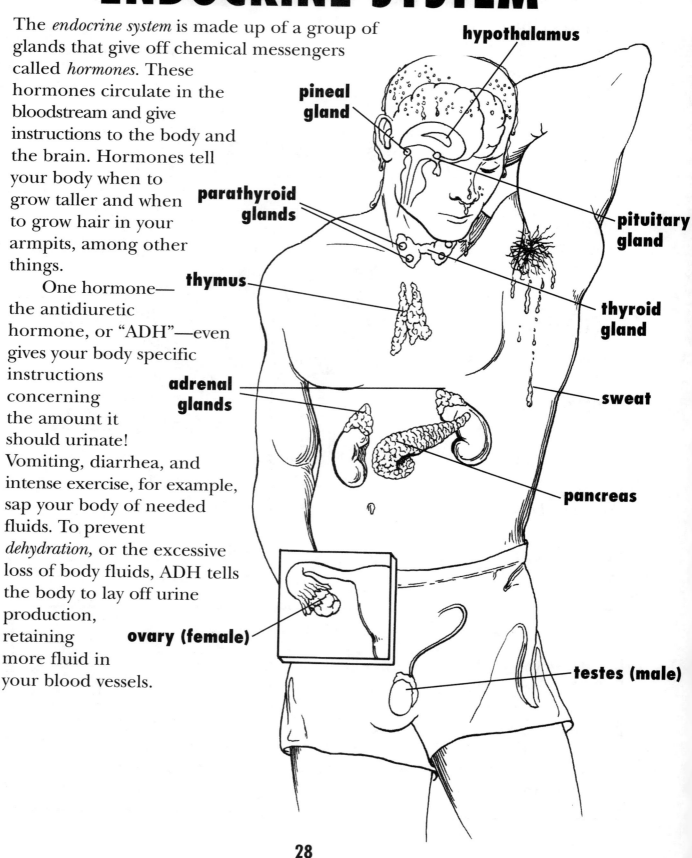

hypothalamus

pineal gland

parathyroid glands

thymus

adrenal glands

ovary (female)

pituitary gland

thyroid gland

sweat

pancreas

testes (male)

The CARDIOVASCULAR SYSTEM

The *cardiovascular system* is composed of the heart and blood vessels that pump blood to every cell in the body. The blood delivers oxygen and nutrients to each cell, and then carries the cell's waste products away to be eliminated.

To meet the cells' needs, the heart circulates blood throughout the blood vessels 24 hours a day, seven days a week, every day of your life.

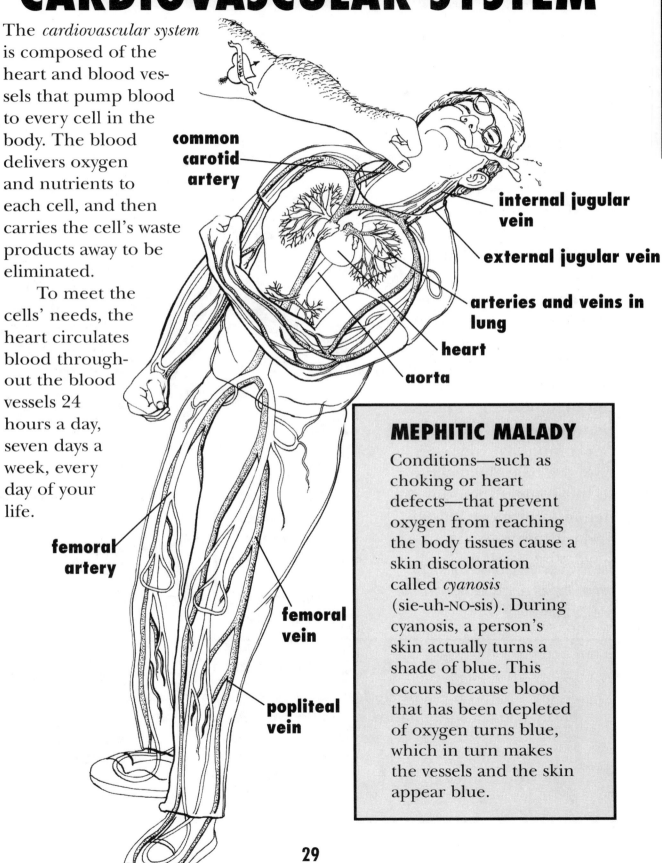

common carotid artery

internal jugular vein

external jugular vein

arteries and veins in lung

heart

aorta

femoral artery

femoral vein

popliteal vein

MEPHITIC MALADY

Conditions—such as choking or heart defects—that prevent oxygen from reaching the body tissues cause a skin discoloration called *cyanosis* (sie-uh-NO-sis). During cyanosis, a person's skin actually turns a shade of blue. This occurs because blood that has been depleted of oxygen turns blue, which in turn makes the vessels and the skin appear blue.

HEART

Although it is only the size of a person's fist, the muscular heart is one hardworking organ. By constantly squeezing and relaxing its muscles, the heart pumps five quarts of blood around the body every *minute*.

Valves between the heart's four chambers open as the heart contracts and shut as it relaxes. These valves ensure the proper path of blood circulation by preventing it from flowing backward. It is the closing of these valves that produces the familiar thumping sound of a heartbeat.

The normal rate for a child's heart to beat is between 70 and 110 times per minute. During exercise, the heart beats faster so it can meet the body's demand for more oxygen and nutrients.

The four separate chambers: the right atrium, the left atrium, the right ventricle, and the left ventricle.

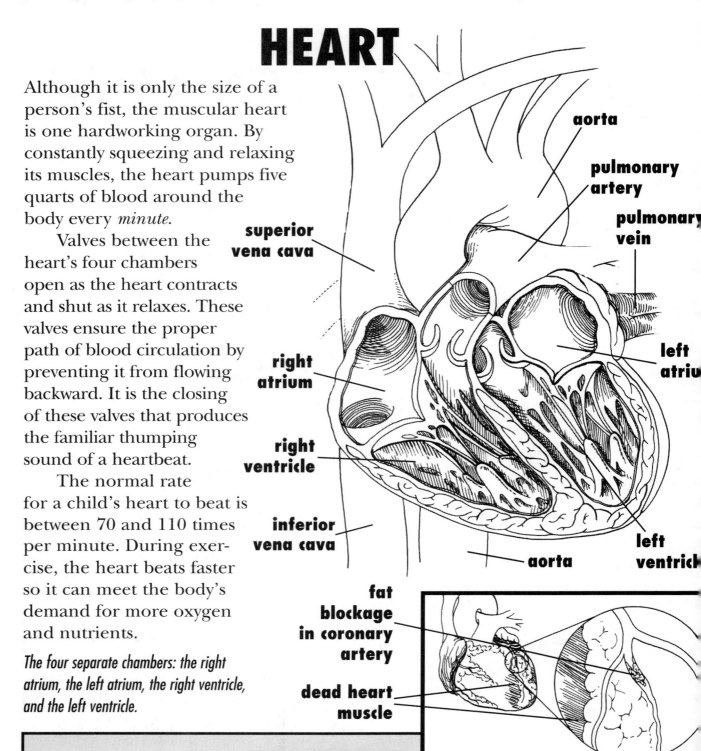

aorta

pulmonary artery

pulmonary vein

superior vena cava

right atrium

left atrium

right ventricle

inferior vena cava

left ventricle

aorta

fat blockage in coronary artery

dead heart muscle

ALL CLOGGED UP

A diet high in fats and cholesterol, stress, and/or a sedentary lifestyle may lead to a disorder called *arteriosclerosis* (ar-TIER-ee-oh-skluh-ROE-sis). In this disorder, fats, cholesterol, and calcium salts deposit themselves on the inner walls of the arteries, causing them to narrow and clog, just like a drainpipe. Arteriosclerosis may result in high blood pressure, a heart attack, a stroke, or even death.

BLOOD

Blood collected in a test tube separates into various parts. The red part of the blood settles to the bottom of the tube, and a clear, yellowish liquid floats above the red material.

The red blood cells, called *erythrocytes* (ih-RITH-ruh-sites), found on the bottom of the test tube make up 44 percent of the blood. Hemoglobin contained in these red blood cells carries oxygen from the lungs to the body cells.

Right above the red blood cells is a thin layer of white blood cells and *platelets* (PLATE-lets). Although they make up a tiny fraction of the blood (less than 1 percent), white blood cells and platelets possess important duties. Five different types of white blood cells, called *leukocytes* (LOO-kuh-sites), help to fight off infections and germs in the body. Platelets help to clot, or clump, the blood so that the bleeding from a wound, such as a cut or scrape, stops before you bleed to death.

Plasma accounts for almost 55 percent of our blood. This clear, yellowish liquid is made up of water, proteins, fats, gases, and sugar. Plasma is responsible for carrying away waste from cells for final elimination via urine or sweat.

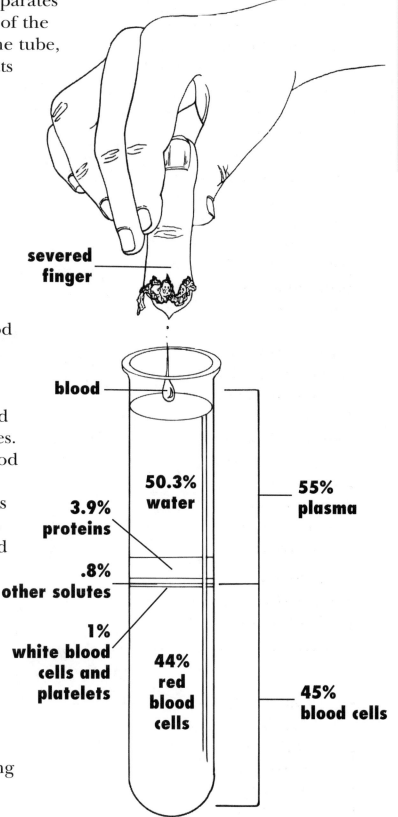

severed finger

blood

3.9% proteins

50.3% water

55% plasma

.8% other solutes

1% white blood cells and platelets

44% red blood cells

45% blood cells

31

ARTERIES AND VEINS

The heart pumps blood through a system of blood vessels. The different types of blood vessels include arteries, arterioles, capillaries, venules, and veins.

   Arteries (AR-tuh-reez) are the thick-walled, elastic blood vessels that carry newly re-oxygenated blood away from the heart to the rest of the body. As they get farther away from the heart, the arteries narrow into thin branches called *arterioles* (ar-TIER-ee-ohlz). Arterioles narrow into even smaller vessels, called *capillaries* (KAP-uh-lair-eez). It is through the thin capillary walls that oxygen and carbon dioxide, as well as nutrients and wastes, are exchanged between the blood and the body's cells.

   The blood, now depleted of oxygen and carrying waste, flows into slim blood vessels, or *venules* (VEN-yoolz). The venules widen into veins. Because the veins carry oxygen-depleted blood, these vessels appear to be a bluish green color when you look at the skin.

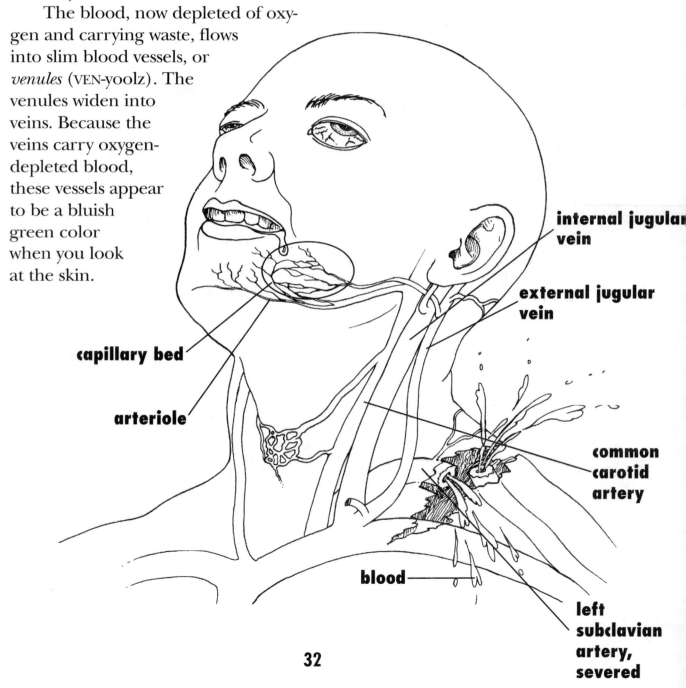

internal jugular vein

external jugular vein

capillary bed

arteriole

common carotid artery

blood

left subclavian artery, severed

VARICOSE VEINS

Twisted and bulging veins in the lower trunk or legs are known as *varicose* (VAIR-ih-kohs) *veins*. All veins have valves that are supposed to prevent blood from flowing backward. If the valves fail to work properly, veins bloat with backed-up blood, causing varicose veins.

Poor posture, prolonged standing, pregnancy, and obesity all put added pressure on the valves and cause the veins to stretch, possibly leading to varicosities. Because pregnancy and higher rates of obesity occur in women, females are more prone to develop varicose veins.

In more severe cases, doctors will sometimes surgically remove a portion of the varicose vein.

great saphenous vein

small saphenous vein

varicose veins

femoral vein

femur

leech

vein

suture

DISGUSTING DOCTORING

If an appendage, like an ear or a finger, has been cut, chopped, or torn off, doctors may try to surgically reattach the part by reconnecting the severed blood vessels. To aid in this procedure, doctors sometimes enlist the help of leeches.

Surgeons apply the bloodsucking worms to the severed appendage. The creatures bite into the tissue and secrete *hirudin* (hih-RUDE-in), a substance that helps to re-open the veins. Although the leech drops off when it has drunk its fill of blood, the bite site continues to ooze blood, improving the venous circulation and thus keeping the appendage alive until it is fully reattached to the body.

the LYMPHATIC SYSTEM

The *lymphatic system* is made up of organs, tissues, and tubelike vessels designed to defend the body against harmful germs. By filtering the air and producing white blood cells that devour bacteria, the structures of this system provide *immunity* (ih-MYOO-nih-tee), which means resistance to infection and disease.

The lymphatic system also manufactures, filters, and circulates a thin, watery fluid called *lymph* (limf). The lymph contains body fluids, blood cells, and liquid fats, called *chyle* (kile), and delivers nutrients to the body and collects waste from cells.

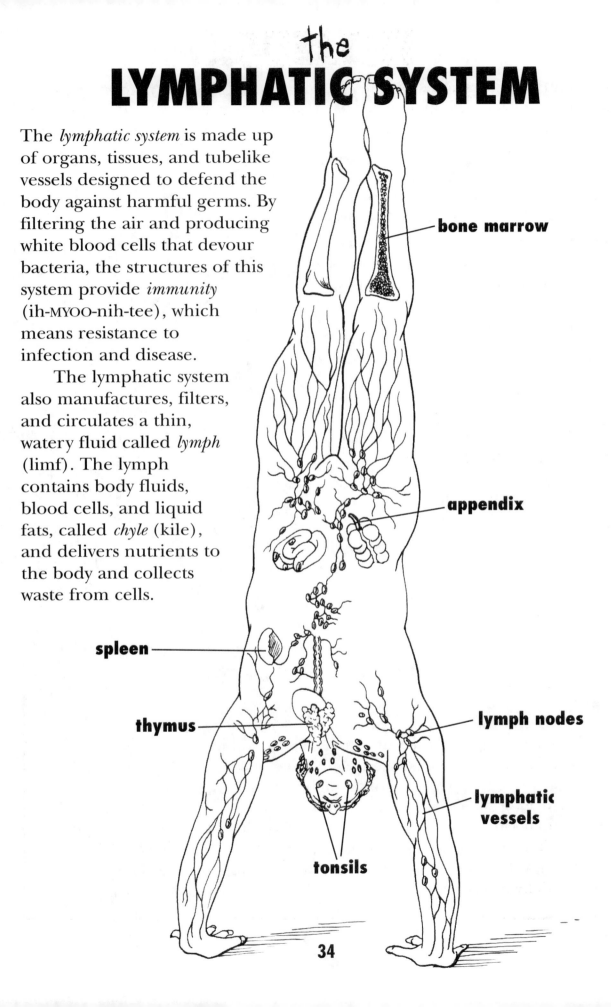

bone marrow

appendix

spleen

thymus

lymph nodes

lymphatic vessels

tonsils

THYMUS

The main organ of the lymphatic system is the *thymus*. This flat, elongated organ is located in the neck. Scientists believe that throughout a person's lifetime, the thymus breaks off little chunks of itself and sends them to other sites in the body. These migrating thymus cells will transform into new lymph nodes or spleen cells, depending on their destination.

The thymus also produces *lymphocytes* (LIM-fuh-sites), a type of white blood cell known as the body's "killer cells." Lymphocytes demolish germs in the lymph fluid by poisoning them with chemicals.

Normally a pinkish color, the thymus is largest during the teenage years. As humans age, the thymus shrivels up into a yellow lump of fat.

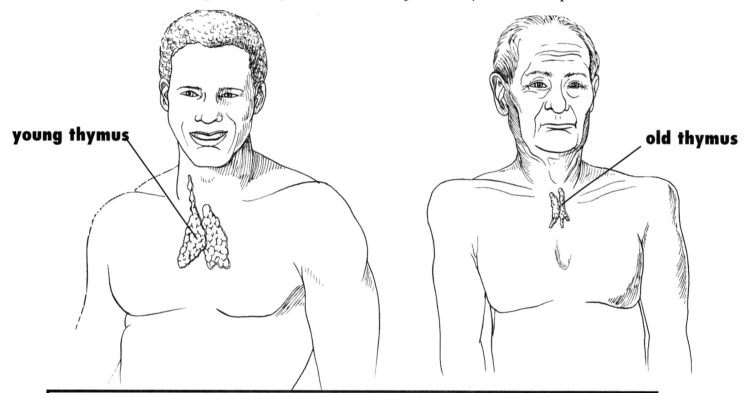

young thymus

old thymus

FOUL PHAGOCYTOSIS

When *macrophages* (MACK-ruh-fayj-uhz)—certain types of white blood cells—detect bacteria or foreign substances in the body, they engulf these infectious bodies and digest them. The entire process is termed *phagocytosis* (fag-uh-sie-TOE-sis).

Infectious bodies do not go down without a fight, however. Bacteria can destroy and liquefy the macrophage militia, producing a gooey, yellowish green substance called *pus*. Pus is a thick, potentially foul-smelling fluid, made up dead white blood cells.

SPLEEN

While scientists know that the *spleen* produces and stores blood cells, their research on this purple-colored organ continues. Many scientists believe that the spleen may take care of other functions for the body that have not yet been discovered. The spleen is composed of both red and white spongy tissue called *pulp*.

The plentiful red pulp destroys old and/or injured red blood cells. Mixed in with the red pulp are smaller patches of white pulp. In the white pulp regions, lymphocytes are manufactured and stored. These lymphocytes help to destroy microorganisms in the spleen.

APPALLING AILMENT

While the normal size of a healthy adult spleen is 2 to 6 pounds, the spleen of a malaria victim may swell to as large as 18½ pounds! Malaria is a parasitic infection transmitted through the bite of a mosquito. When the parasites invade and burst red blood cells, the injured red blood cells that need to be destroyed pour into the spleen, causing it to bulge.

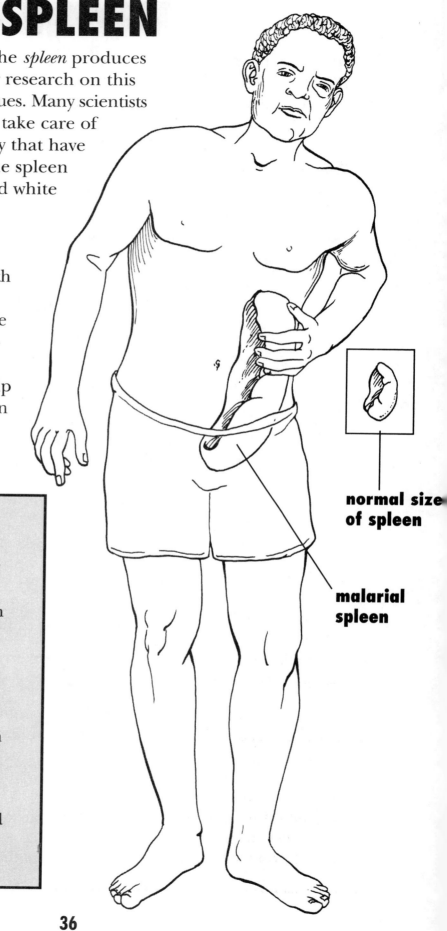

normal size of spleen

malarial spleen

TONSILS

Did you know that you have four pairs of *tonsils* in your throat? These pink bulbous mounds of flesh police the respiratory tract. They screen inhaled air for disease-causing organisms, and trap the invading culprits until they can be devoured by the immune system.

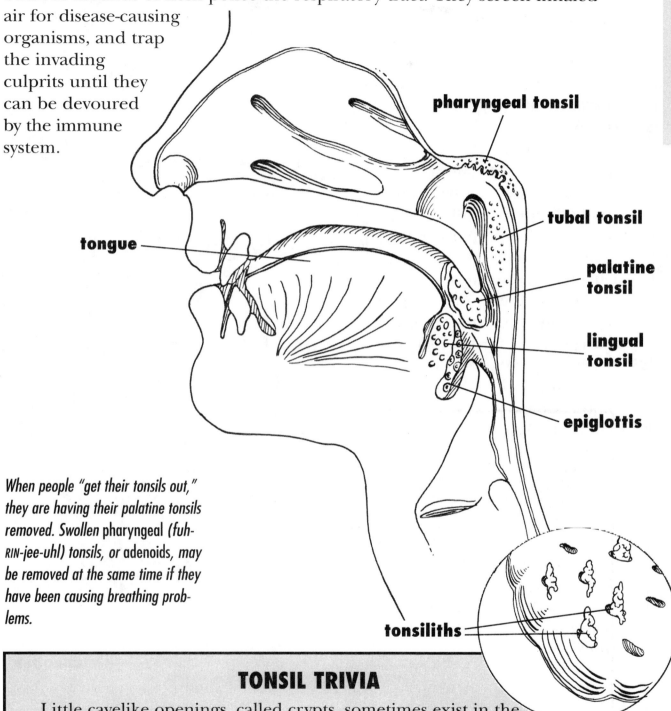

tongue

pharyngeal tonsil

tubal tonsil

palatine tonsil

lingual tonsil

epiglottis

tonsiliths

When people "get their tonsils out," they are having their palatine tonsils removed. Swollen pharyngeal *(fuh-RIN-jee-uhl) tonsils, or adenoids, may be removed at the same time if they have been causing breathing problems.*

TONSIL TRIVIA

Little cavelike openings, called crypts, sometimes exist in the palatine tonsils. Food, saliva, mucus, and bacteria can collect in these crypts, where they harden and form foul-smelling yellow tonsil boogers, called *tonsiliths* (TAHN-sul-iths).

LYMPHATIC VESSELS

Lymphatic vessels first absorb liquids and proteins that normally ooze out of the capillaries. This fluid becomes part of the lymph, and it is filtered as it circulates through the thin, transparent vessels of the lymphatic system. This fluid eventually goes back into the bloodstream.

Two *lymphatic ducts* in the neck spew out about 4 ounces of lymph per hour into the bloodstream. During intense exercise, lymph may gush at a rate of 80 ounces (a little more than a 2-liter bottle of soda) per hour through these ducts and back into the blood vessels.

Without lymphatic vessels to return fluids to the bloodstream, people would puff up and their skin would feel like mashed potatoes. Fluid might drip through the skin. If the excess fluids pooled around the heart or lungs, death could quickly result.

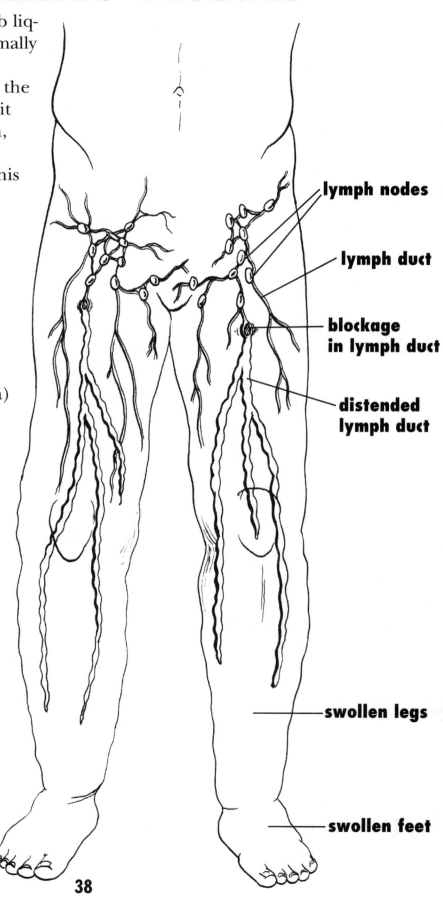

lymph nodes

lymph duct

blockage
in lymph duct

distended
lymph duct

swollen legs

swollen feet

LYMPH NODES

Lymph nodes can be as small as pinheads or as large as lima beans. Clusters of these nodes are located in the neck, groin, abdomen, and armpits.

Preventing infection is the main duty of the lymph nodes. When bacteria enter the body, the egg-shaped nodes filter out the germs from the lymph. This prevents the bacteria from entering the bloodstream and multiplying.

The lymph nodes also manufacture two different types of white blood cells, *lymphocytes* (LIM-fuh-sites) and *monocytes* (MAH-nuh-sites). Like all white blood cells, the lymphocytes and monocytes kill germs that invade the body.

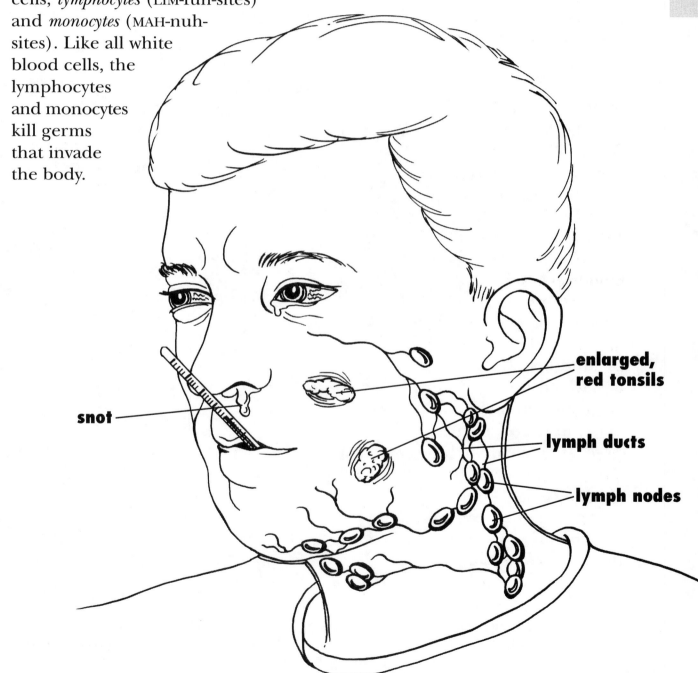

snot

enlarged, red tonsils

lymph ducts

lymph nodes

the RESPIRATORY SYSTEM

The *respiratory tract* provides the human body with the oxygen it needs to survive. As air is inhaled into the lungs, the oxygen in the air is circulated throughout the bloodstream so it can be used by the body. When we exhale, the respiratory tract lets out the body's gaseous waste product, *carbon dioxide.*

The two sections of the respiratory system, the upper tract and the lower tract, each serve a different purpose. The upper respiratory tract includes everything from the nasal cavity to the *trachea* (TRAY-key-uh), or windpipe. It acts to warm, filter, and humidify the inhaled air. The lower tract, made up of the *bronchi* (BRONG-key) and the lungs, has the role of exchanging the oxygen that we breathe in for the carbon dioxide that we breathe out.

Follow a breathful of germs as they work their way through the respiratory tract.

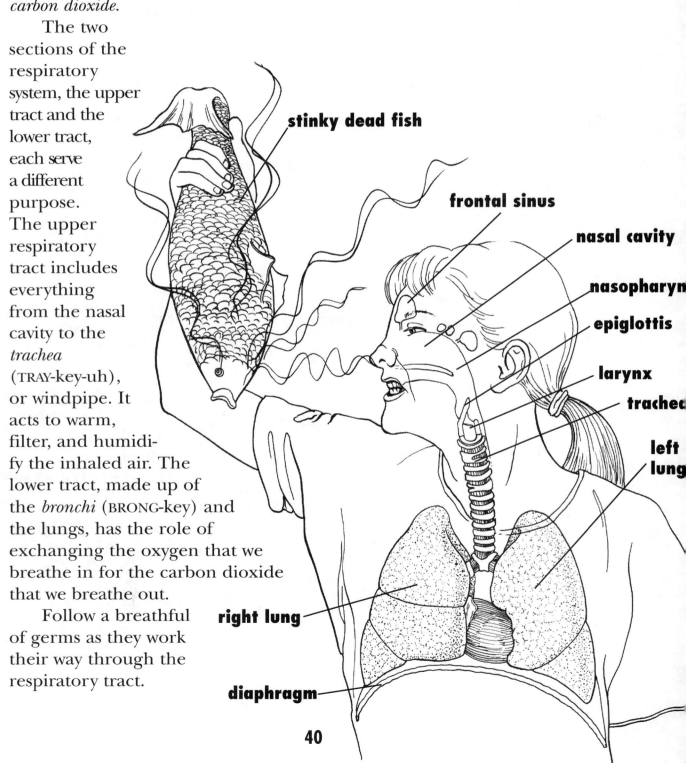

stinky dead fish

frontal sinus

nasal cavity

nasopharynx

epiglottis

larynx

trachea

left lung

right lung

diaphragm

40

NASAL CAVITIES

The nasal cavities are the spaces just inside the nose through which air passes.

When someone sneezes, thousands of tiny droplets containing snot, saliva, and potentially infectious germs spray into the airspace of everyone within 3 to 5 feet. These contaminated droplets are now free to gain entry into an unsuspecting person's respiratory tract through the mouth and nostrils. These droplets may either be breathed in or put into the person's mouth and nostrils by a contaminated finger or hand.

The germs flow into the right and left nasal cavities inside the nostrils, where bristly hairs that line these passages, called *cilia* (SILL-ee-uh), immediately halt some of the inhaled intruders. The *serous* (SEER-us) *glands*, found in the lining of the nose, immediately start working to secrete a thick, gooey mucus that traps the foreign particles so that these particles may later be removed from the nose by either blowing, sneezing, or picking.

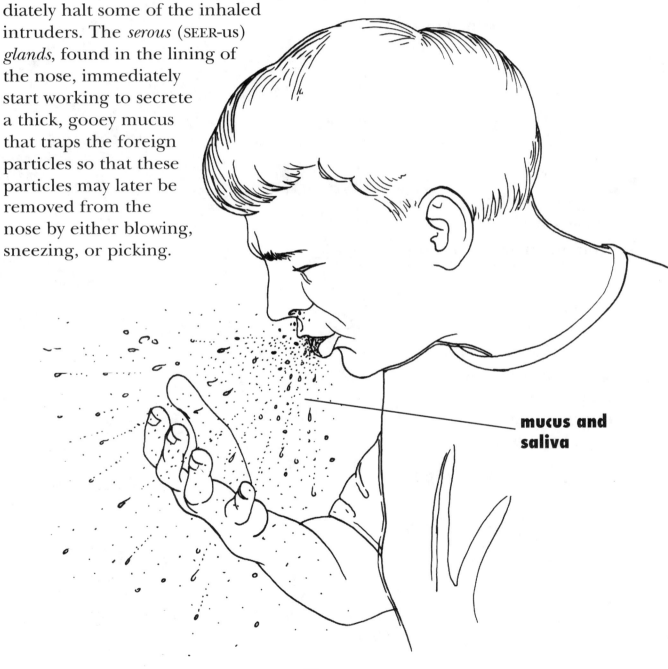

mucus and
saliva

SINUSES

Humans have four pairs of mucus-lined *paranasal sinuses* (pahr-uh-NAY-zul SIE-nuhs-iz), which are air-filled pockets in the bones around the nose. The sinuses trap and expel foreign matter, using the nasal cavities to drain their secretions.

Because the sinuses share part of their mucous membranes with the nose, germ droplets that were not trapped by the nose hairs may enter the sinuses. These germs can cause enough irritation and swelling in your passageways to block the normal discharge of the sinuses. These secretions build up in the sinus cavity, allowing the invading germs to flourish and develop an infection.

At this point, *sinusitis,* swelling of the sinus, occurs. Thick yellowish green sinus secretions may ooze into the nose and throat. The face or forehead over the infected sinus may become swollen and red. Severe sinus infections can even spread into the surrounding bones or into the brain.

frontal sinus

maxillary sinus

esophagus

epiglottis close over trachea

trachea

42

LARYNX

The upper and lower respiratory tracts are connected by the *larynx* (LAR-inks). The larynx, or voice box, produces sound. It is shaped like a cylinder and is made up of cartilage held together by ligaments. The bulging thyroid cartilage is often called the Adam's apple.

When a germ droplet or other foreign debris irritates the larynx, it produces the cough reflex—the second function of this organ. Coughing helps rid the larynx and throat of foreign particles by hacking them back into the air.

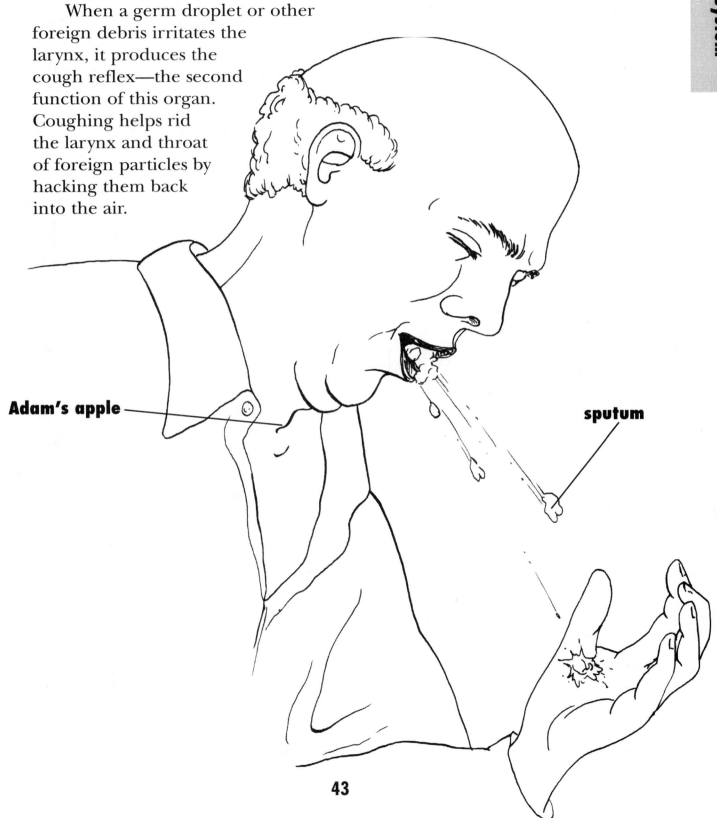

Adam's apple

sputum

43

EPIGLOTTIS

The *epiglottis* (ep-ih-GLOT-is) is a little piece of cartilage that acts as a lid, covering the larynx and trachea when we eat or drink. It prevents us from choking to death when we swallow food or fluid.

The epiglottis also attempts to prevent infectious sinus and nasal discharge from entering your lower respiratory tract. It sometimes fails, however, allowing infections of the lower tract or *pneumonia* (new-MOAN-yuh) to develop.

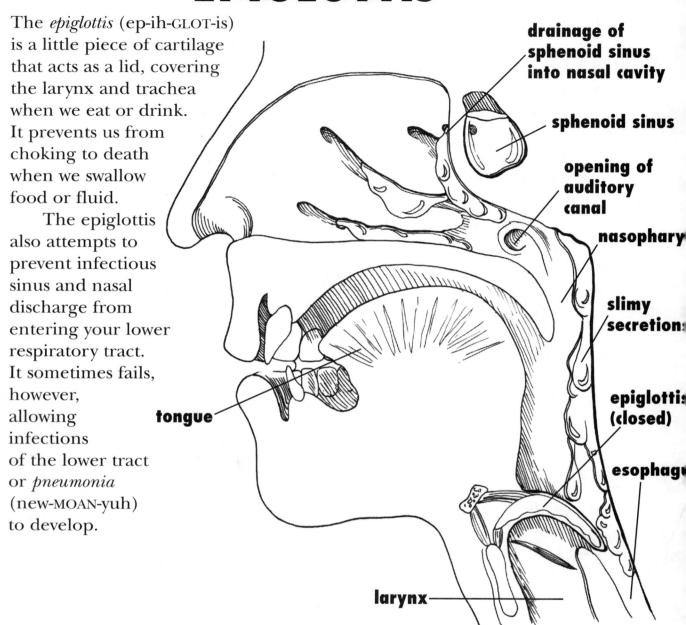

drainage of sphenoid sinus into nasal cavity

sphenoid sinus

opening of auditory canal

nasophary

slimy secretion

epiglotti (closed)

esophagu

tongue

larynx

TORMENTING TREATMENT

If infected by bacteria, the epiglottis may become severely swollen, cutting off the air supply to the lungs. When this swelling presents a life-or-death situation, physicians have been known to stab needles, scalpels, and even ballpoint pens into a patient's trachea to save his or her life! The surgical process of spearing a hole into the trachea is called a *tracheotomy* (tray-key-OTT-uh-me), and it allows oxygen into the otherwise blocked airway.

TRACHEA

The *trachea* delivers oxygen to your lungs. The tubelike trachea resembles a vacuum cleaner hose because it is surrounded by rings of cartilage. These cartilage rings prevent the trachea from collapsing while you inhale.

To prevent intruding organisms from entering the lungs, the slippery lining of your trachea coats most germs with *phlegm*, a thick, slimy mucus.

Tiny hairlike projections in your trachea, called *cilia*, are constantly moving back and forth. Their waving action sweeps the phlegm back up into your throat, where it is swallowed, or coughed up and spit out.

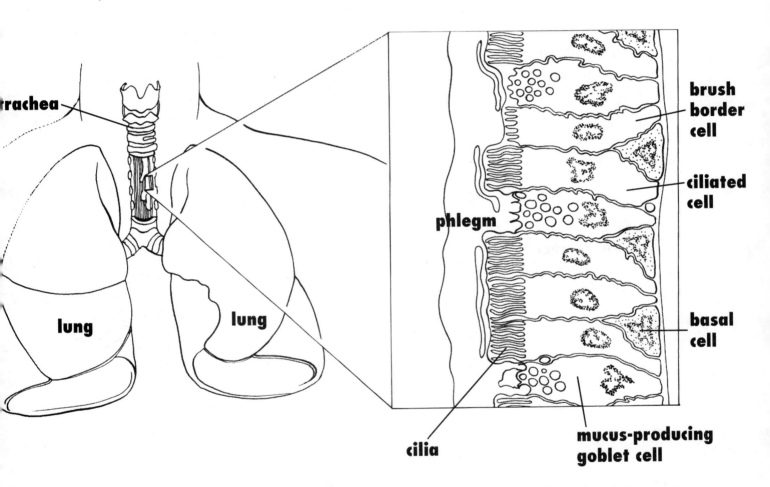

trachea

lung

lung

phlegm

cilia

brush border cell

ciliated cell

basal cell

mucus-producing goblet cell

MORE ON MUCUS

Phlegm that you *expectorate* (eck-SPECK-tuh-rate), or cough up and spit out, is called *sputum* (SPEW-tum). If your sputum is green, frothy, bloody, or *purulent* (PURE-yuh-lent) (pus-filled), an infection or disease may be festering in your lungs.

BRONCHI AND LUNGS

The *carina* (kuh-RYE-nuh) is the point at which the trachea branches off into two air passages, the *right bronchus* and *left bronchus*. Each bronchus enters a lung through a slit called a *hilum* (HIGH-lum). The right lung contains three lobes, or sections, and the left lung contains two.

The dark pinkish red cone-shaped lungs are the breathing organs in the respiratory tract. Smooth and shiny on the outside and spongy on the inside, your lungs inflate and deflate like balloons every time you inhale and exhale. The lungs' *alveolar* (al-VEE-uh-lur) *sacs* actively exchange oxygen for carbon dioxide.

Microorganisms that reach the lungs may either be killed by your body's immune system or begin multiplying in the lungs, causing a cold, flu, infection, or *pneumonia* (new-MOAN-yuh). The alveoli in a person suffering from pneumonia become filled with fluid or gummy pockets of pus. The affected lobes of the lung become firm and fluid-filled, causing fits of coughing.

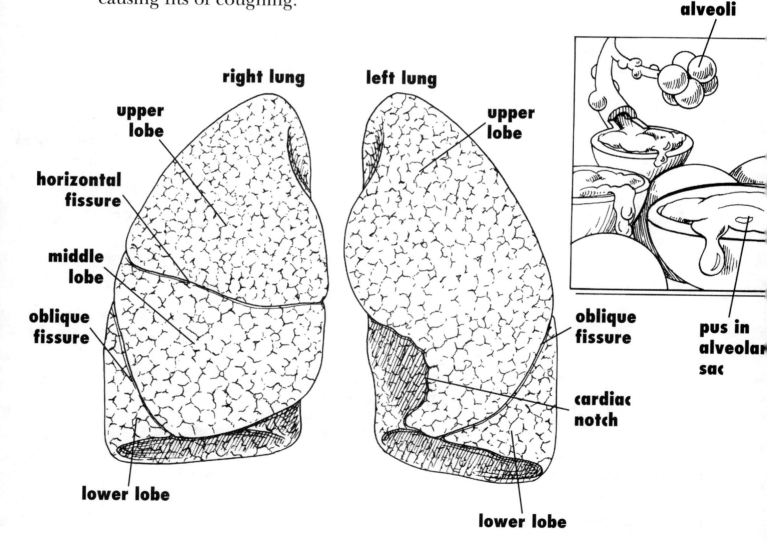

right lung

left lung

upper lobe

upper lobe

horizontal fissure

middle lobe

oblique fissure

oblique fissure

cardiac notch

alveoli

pus in alveolar sac

lower lobe

lower lobe

46

SMOKER'S LUNGS

Each time a smoker takes a drag on a cigarette, the hot smoke irritates and dries out the tissues of the mouth, larynx, trachea, and lungs. Thousands of chemicals that are poisonous to the human body are inhaled with each puff. These chemicals are proven to cause many illnesses, including lung cancer, a deadly disease that rapidly eats away at the healthy tissues of the lungs.

One of the dirtiest chemicals contained in cigarettes is a sticky, dark brown substance called tar. This tar, which leaves a thick, dark coating on a person's lungs, is similar to the type used to pave roads.

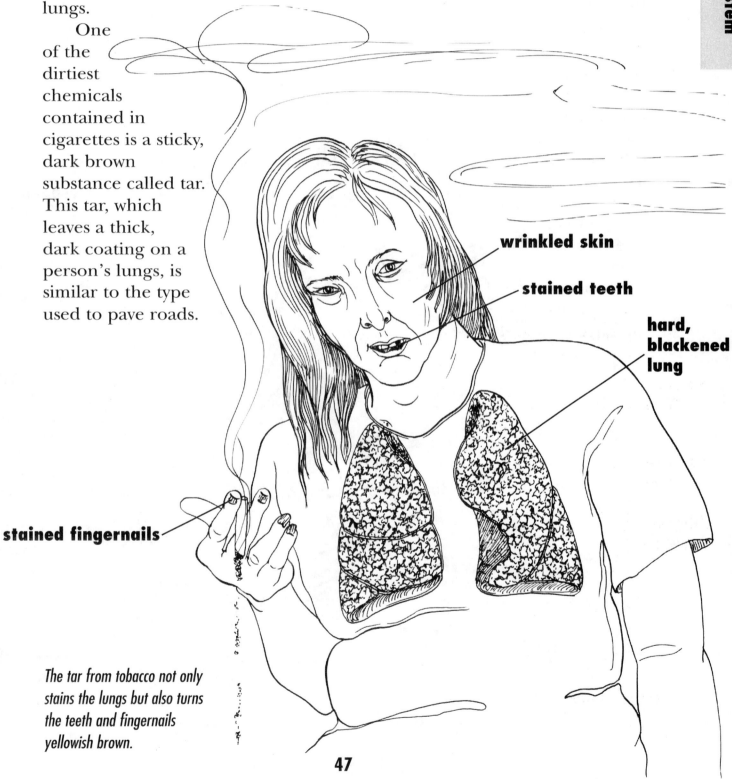

wrinkled skin

stained teeth

hard, blackened lung

stained fingernails

The tar from tobacco not only stains the lungs but also turns the teeth and fingernails yellowish brown.

47

The DIGESTIVE SYSTEM

The *alimentary* (al-uh-MEN-tuh-ree) canal runs from the mouth to the anus via the throat, esophagus, stomach, small and large intestines, and rectum. These are the organs of the digestive system, and they change what you eat from food to feces.

Follow a slice of pizza through the digestive tract and see how a food so marvelous turns into a thing so malodorous.

Although the liver, gallbladder, and pancreas are not parts of the alimentary canal, they are considered accessory (helper) organs to the digestive system.

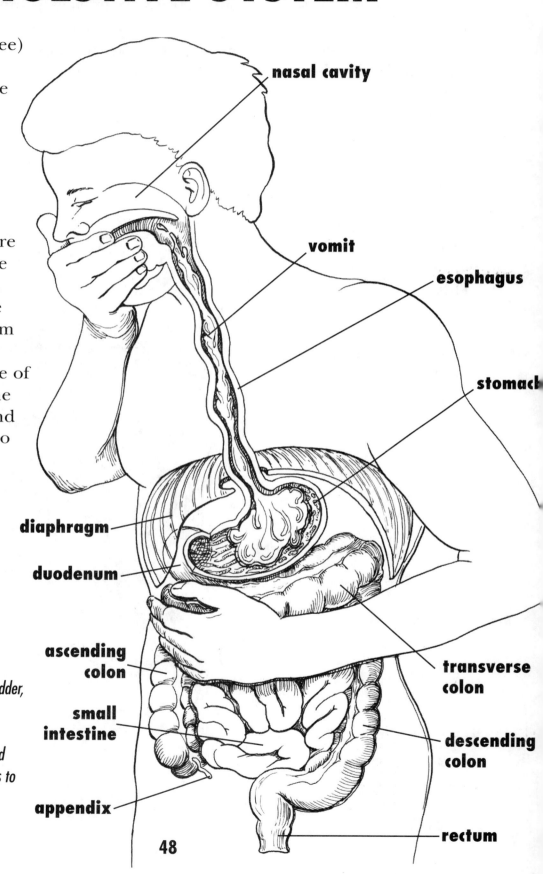

nasal cavity

vomit

esophagus

stomach

diaphragm

duodenum

ascending colon

small intestine

appendix

transverse colon

descending colon

rectum

SALIVARY GLANDS

When the thought or smell of a slice of pizza starts your mouth watering, your *salivary* (SAL-uh-ver-ee) *glands* are actually mass-producing saliva in preparation for digesting it.

Proteins in the saliva, called *enzymes* (EN-zimez), start breaking down the starches in the pizza shortly after you put it into your mouth. Saliva also lubricates the pizza for its journey down the esophagus.

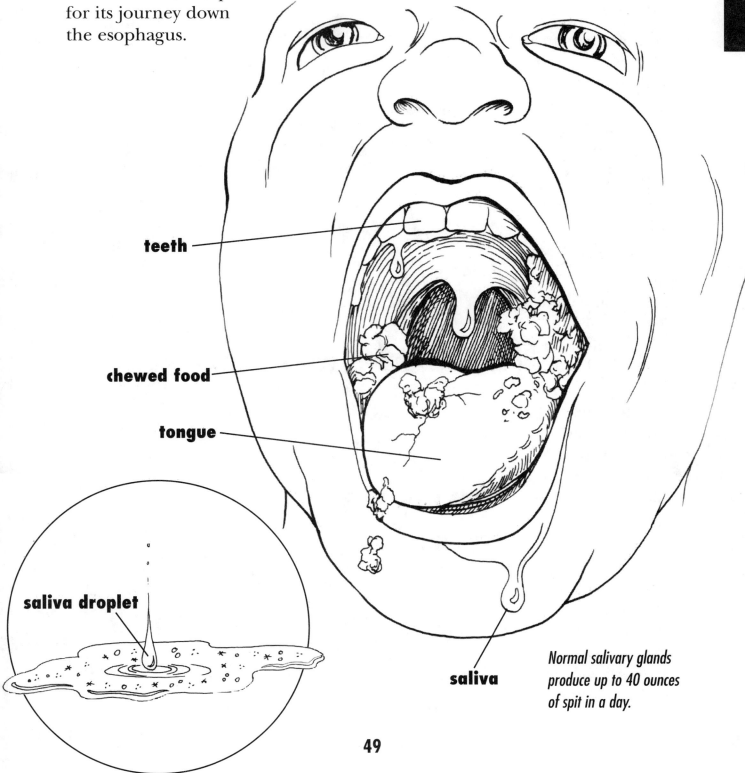

teeth

chewed food

tongue

saliva droplet

saliva

Normal salivary glands produce up to 40 ounces of spit in a day.

49

TEETH

The primary purpose of teeth is to rip, tear, and grind the food that you eat. If you were to thoroughly chew a bite of pizza and open your mouth before swallowing (an experiment best performed in privacy in front of a mirror), you would observe the pizza in a new form. It has become a *bolus* (BOE-lus), or soggy, rounded glob.

When the teeth are not properly brushed and flossed, the buildup of mucus, bacteria, sugars, and food leaves a filmy layer over the teeth called *plaque*. Bacteria cling to the plaque and begin the breakdown of the enamel and then the protein of the teeth, a condition called *dental caries* (dehn-tuhl KARE-ees). Without the care of a dentist, this uncontrolled rotting will leave permanent pits, or *cavities*, in the teeth.

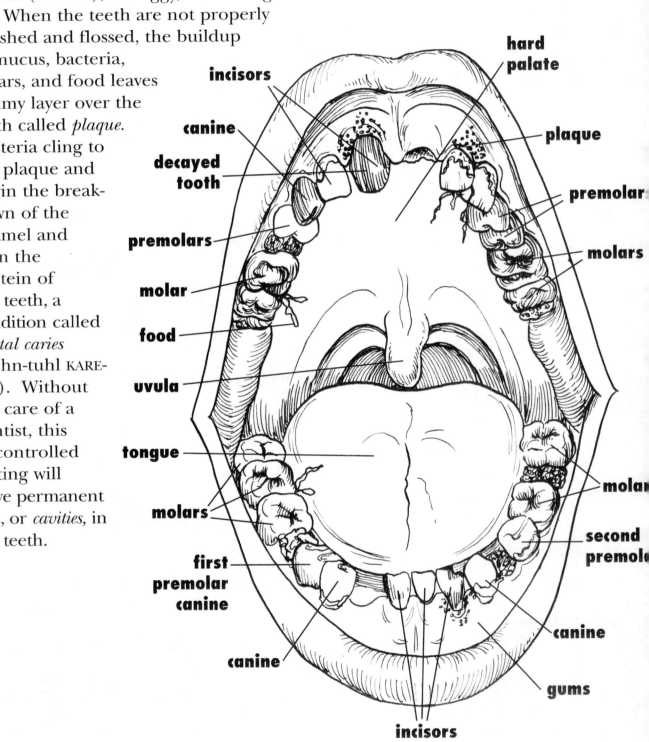

incisors
canine
decayed tooth
premolars
molar
food
uvula
tongue
molars
first premolar canine
canine
incisors

hard palate
plaque
premolars
molars
molar
second premolar
canine
gums

50

TONGUE

A thick muscle covered with mucous membranes, the tongue is used for licking, speaking, and tasting. The tongue also holds food against the teeth during chewing and moves boluses into the throat during swallowing.

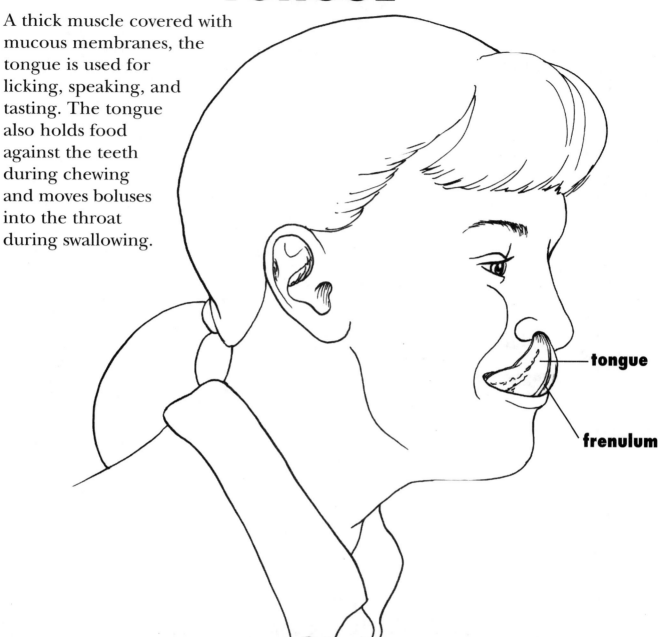

tongue

frenulum

FRENULUM FACT

The distance you can stick your tongue out is determined by your *frenulum* (FREN-yuh-lum), the band of tissue that attaches the tongue to the floor of the mouth.

A short frenulum can make it difficult to pronounce certain words (such as those beginning with the letters T, D, L, or N) and to French-kiss. The cure? Doctors sometimes slice the frenulum with a scalpel to allow for greater tongue flexibility.

ESOPHAGUS

The *esophagus* (ih-SOF-uh-gus) is the ten-inch muscular passageway between the mouth and stomach. Squeezing and relaxing in a wavelike motion, the esophagus moves the food bolus closer and closer to the stomach.

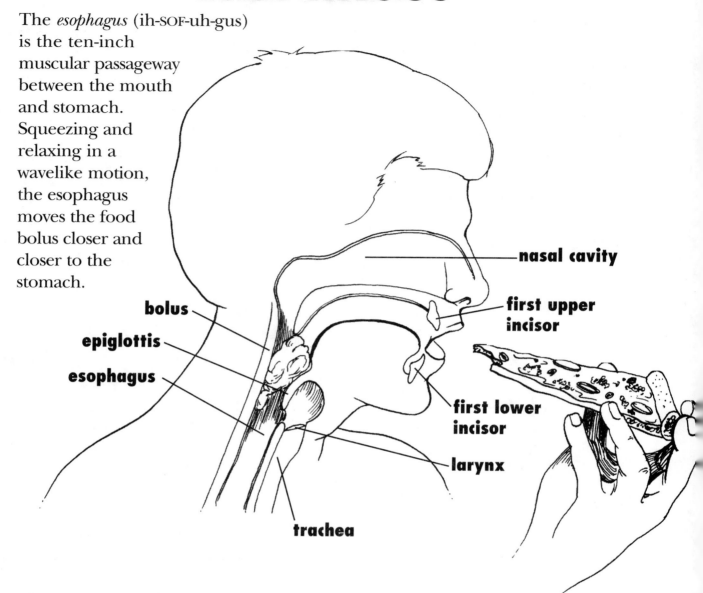

nasal cavity

first upper incisor

bolus

epiglottis

esophagus

first lower incisor

larynx

trachea

AN UP-CLOSE LOOK AT THE UVULA

Look in the mirror and say, "AAAAHHH!" See the mystery meat hanging in the back of your mouth? This dangling flap of flesh is actually a muscle known as the *uvula* (YOU-vyuh-luh). As the bolus travels from the mouth into the esophagus, your uvula swings up to prevent it from going up into your nasal passages.

A warning to those who eat and laugh at the same time: Because laughing prevents the uvula from blocking off the path to your nose, you may shoot a mouthful of chewed food out your nostrils when you crack up in the cafeteria.

STOMACH

When empty, the stomach folds up into little ridges known as *rugae* (ROO-jee) and is about the size of a large sausage. As the pizza boluses drop into the stomach, its walls stretch and contract, squishing and mashing the boluses into a paste.

The lining of the stomach releases *gastric*, or stomach, *enzymes* and acids that begin digesting the proteins in the pizza's cheese. After mixing with these chemicals, the boluses are changed into a thick fluid called *chyme* (kime).

esophagus

bolus

gastric juices

stomach chyme lining

esophagus

baby barf

stomach

VILE VOMITING

Vomiting occurs when the stomach's contents are forcefully expelled up through the esophagus and out the mouth.

Food poisoning, foul odors and tastes, and stomach irritation can all cause vomiting. In addition, some babies and older children force themselves to vomit food back into their mouths, where they can then swallow it again. Doctors believe this voluntary spewing, called *ruminating* (ROO-muh-nate-ing), may be a way for children to excite themselves or to get more attention from their parents.

LIVER

The *liver*'s main role in the digestive process is to make *bile*, which is stored in the gallbladder and used in the small intestine. Each day our livers produce more than 16 ounces of bile, a thick, slimy yellowish green fluid that breaks down fat in the food we eat. As bile passes through the intestines, it becomes darker, giving bowel movements their characteristic brownish color.

Besides making bile, the liver performs over 500 different duties that are essential to the body's healthy survival.

liver

SMALL INTESTINE

It's in this folded section of intestine that most of the digestive process occurs. The *small intestine* actually stretches out to 20 feet in length. This is where the digestion of starches and protein is completed and the complex digestion of fats takes place. As chyme is pushed from the stomach into the small intestine, enzymes and chemicals secreted by the pancreas, liver, and intestines are combined with it.

Although the lining of the small intestine looks smooth, many tiny folds called *plica* (PLY-kuh) appear on its surface. The lining and its folds are covered with *villi* (VILL-eye), millions of microscopic "fingers" that constantly wiggle and wave. Villi absorb nutrients from the chyme as it is slowly pushed through the intestine by a constant squeezing motion. These nutrients are then passed into the blood and lymph to nourish the entire body.

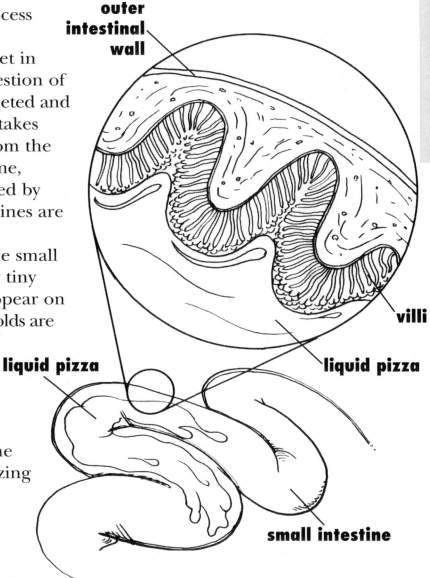

outer intestinal wall

villi

liquid pizza

liquid pizza

small intestine

MEPHITIC MALADY

Stress, alcoholic beverages, and caffeine can cause the stomach to produce too much acid and enzymes. These potent gastric juices gradually wear away the protective mucous membrane lining of the esophagus, intestine, and stomach, creating holes called *ulcers*.

Gastric acids and enzymes begin leaking out of these ulcers and into the abdominal cavity, where most of the digestive organs are located. There, the acids begin literally frying the tissue like bacon in a skillet. Severe ulcers can cause a person to bleed to death.

LARGE INTESTINE

The *large intestine* performs the final removal of fluids from the chyme. As liquids are absorbed into the intestinal lining, the chyme is transformed into a solid mass called *feces* (FEE-seez). Feces are made up of undigested food, cellulose, dead cells, mucus, and bacteria.

Within every healthy person's large intestine, harmless bacteria live and breed. These germs actually help us by aiding in the production of vitamin K, which is essential to the clotting of blood. The bacteria also produce the malodorous gases expelled as *flatus* (FLAY-tus), or farts.

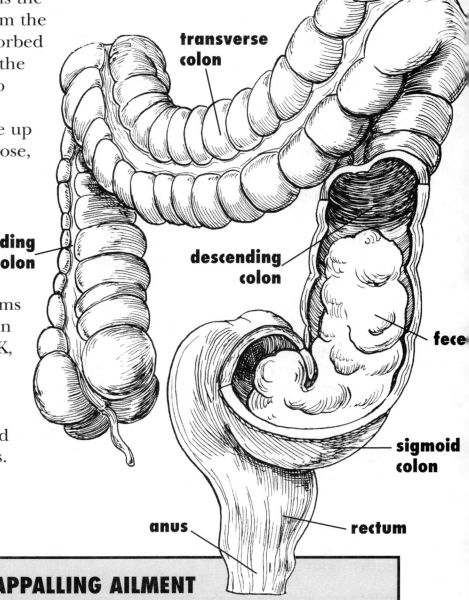

transverse colon

ascending colon

descending colon

fece

sigmoid colon

anus

rectum

APPALLING AILMENT

The entire process of digestion—from mouth to anus—usually takes 18 to 30 hours. *Constipation* occurs when feces is held in the large intestine for longer than this normal time. The longer the feces stays in the large intestine, the more fluid is absorbed into the body. This makes the feces harder and more difficult to pass through the rectum.

There are instances when a person becomes so crammed full of feces that his or her breath smells of stool, a medical condition known as *feculent breath.* In extreme cases, people have actually vomited feces.

RECTUM

The *rectum* is the final holding station for feces before they are expelled from the anus. About 5 inches long, the rectum is located at the end of the large intestine. As it fills with feces, the nerves in the rectum send a message to the brain, urging you to evacuate the load as soon as possible.

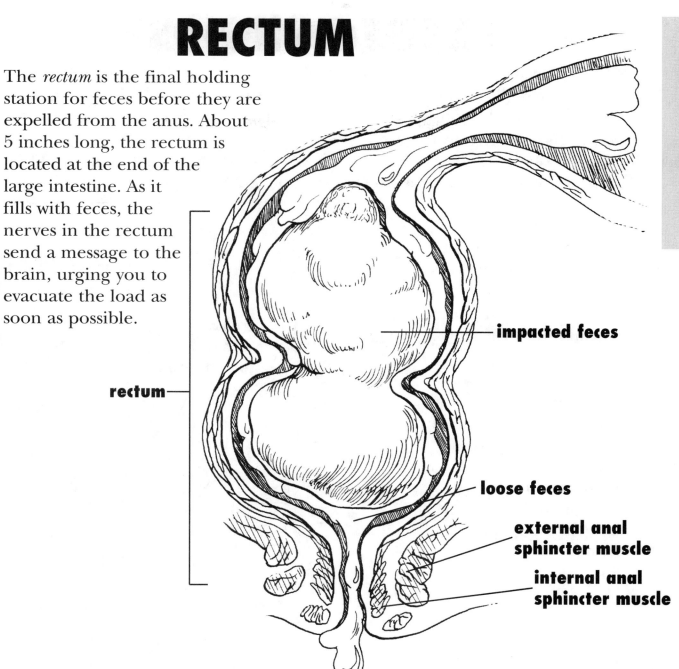

rectum

impacted feces

loose feces

external anal sphincter muscle

internal anal sphincter muscle

FOUL FECAL BLOCKAGE

Hard pieces of old feces can get lodged in the rectum, even though other pieces may be passing through. If none of the feces can pass, medication or enemas may be prescribed to loosen and expel the blockage.

If those treatments fail, a physician may need to perform a *manual evacuation*. In this procedure, a doctor must insert his or her finger into the person's rectum to free the fecal jam.

HEMORRHOIDS

Commonly found in the rectal and anal areas are *hemorrhoids* (HEM-uh-roidz), veins that swell and protrude with an extra supply of blood. Hemorrhoids may be caused by constipation, straining during bowel movements or childbirth, or obesity.

Although hemorrhoids are rarely dangerous, they are uncomfortable and may itch or bleed when feces are expelled. To relieve the pain of hemorrhoids, doctors may recommend an over-the-counter ointment (such as Preparation H), hot or cold compresses, sitz baths (soaking in warm water), or *ligation* (lie-GAY-shun).

During a ligation, a doctor grabs and pulls a hemorrhoid with forceps, then tightly secures a special type of rubber band around its base. Within approximately a week, the hemorrhoidal tissue shrivels up and falls off.

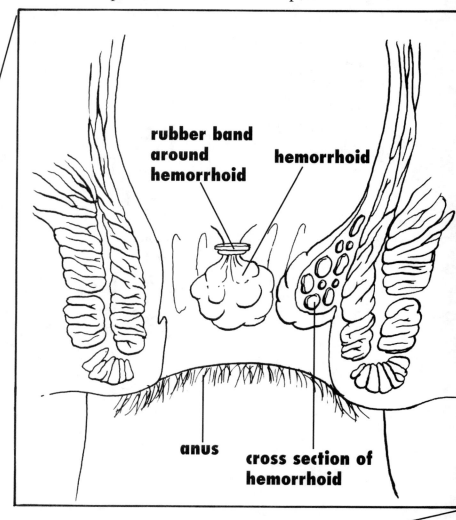

rubber band around hemorrhoid

hemorrhoid

anus

cross section of hemorrhoid

ANUS

The *anus* is the exit of the alimentary canal. A circular band of muscle fibers, called the *anal sphincter*, pulls the anus closed tight except when it is passing feces—which happens between one to three times per day.

During toilet training, children are taught how to control their sphincter muscles.

Fissures (FISH-urz), the name given to cracks in the skin, are fairly common in the anus. They may be caused by constipation, straining during bowel movements, the friction of wiping too hard with toilet paper, or trauma to the anus.

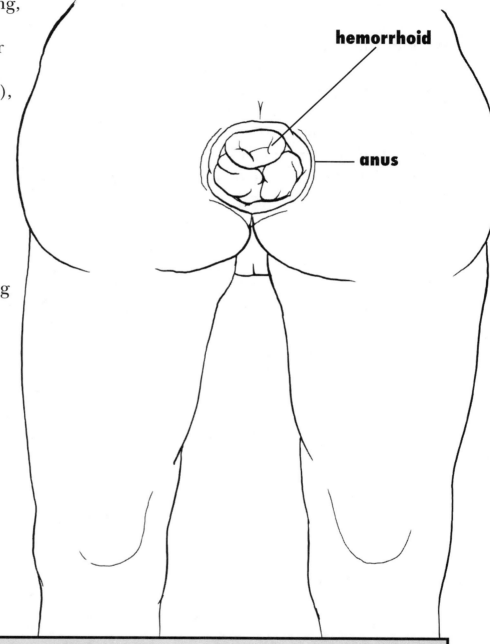

hemorrhoid

anus

GROSS GLOSSARY

Dingleberry: A dingleberry is the slang term for a small, sticky piece of stool that requires twitching, shaking, bouncing, or plucking to detach it from your anus.

The URINARY SYSTEM

The *urinary system* filters the blood and helps maintain the proper balance of fluids and chemicals in the body. It also excretes the body's liquid wastes, just as the digestive system eliminates solid waste. Made up of two kidneys, two *ureters* (you-REE-turz), a bladder, and a *urethra* (you-REE-thruh), the urinary tract is sometimes described as the body's plumbing.

A cool, refreshing glass of cranberry juice ends up as a warm stream of urine in about 1 to 4 hours. Follow the cranberry juice as it is filtered and resorbed by the urinary system!

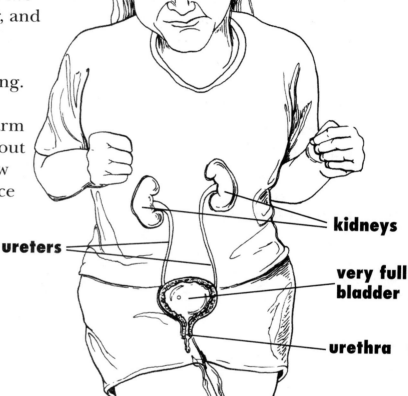

kidneys

ureters

very full bladder

urethra

urine

swollen, puckering legs

BLOWN-UP BODIES

Without a properly functioning urinary tract, the body retains the fluid and salts that are normally excreted as urine. The body then becomes bloated and swollen like a balloon. This condition is known as *edema* (ih-DEE-muh).

KIDNEYS

The bean-shaped *kidneys* contain millions of tiny *nephrons* (NEF-ronz), which act as filters to remove waste, excess fluids, and salts from your body. The kidneys secrete these products into a fluid called *urine*. Although nearly everyone is born with two kidneys, a person can survive with only one.

After your digestive tract absorbed the vitamins and nutrients from the cranberry juice, most of the fluid was resorbed into your bloodstream. Along with every other drop of blood in your body, the fluid from your juice will then make twenty trips through your kidneys in an hour.

Through a process of straining and filtering, the kidneys either retain or excrete the body's fluids. So as most of the fluids from the juice is returned to your bloodstream, the rest of it is sent dribbling away as urine.

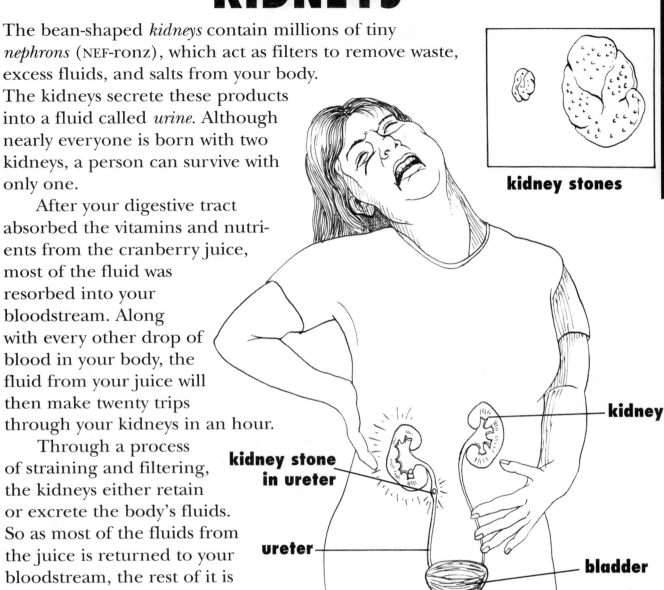

kidney stones

kidney stone in ureter

kidney

ureter

bladder

urethra

MEPHITIC MALADY

Disease, breakdown of bone tissue, and infections may cause *calculi* (KAL-kyuh-lie), or stones, to develop in the urinary tract. Usually made up of calcium, these pebblelike masses appear most often in the kidney. Stones may block urine flow and cause infections or permanent damage.

As the stones move through the urinary tract, they cause excruciating pain. Patients have described having stones as feeling as if "a bowling ball was trying to pass through" them.

URETERS

When the juice-now-turned-urine is ready to leave the kidney, it is pushed down two 12-inch-long drainage tubes called *ureters* (you-REE-turz). The mucus-lined ureters connect the kidneys to the bladder.

The muscles of the ureters squeeze several times each minute to pump urine into the bladder, in the same way that the intestines squeeze stool through to the rectum.

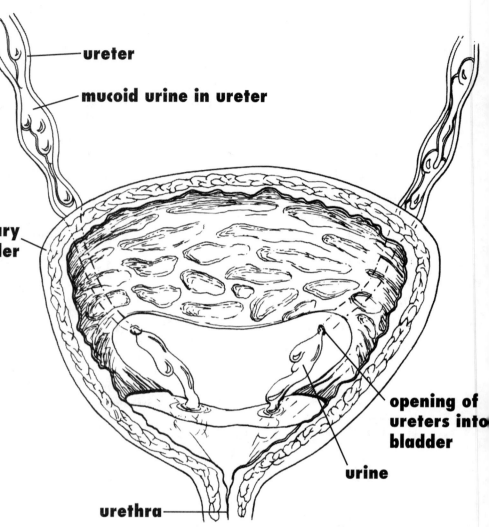

ureter

mucoid urine in ureter

urinary bladder

opening of ureters into bladder

urine

urethra

EXECRABLE EXCRETIONS

When a person's kidneys progressively fail, urea (a compound made from ammonia and carbon dioxide) and other waste products build up in the blood because the production of healthy urine stops. Since these waste products cannot be excreted through the urinary tract, the body tries to find a way to eliminate them. The waste products seep through the capillaries and appear as a pale crust of white crystals on the skin. These deposits, called *uremic frost,* are a clear physical symptom of irreversible kidney damage.

In spite of this effort to rid the blood of waste buildup, a person whose kidneys fail will fall into a coma and die without proper medical treatments.

BLADDER

The *bladder* is a muscular sac that acts as the holding tank for the urinary system. Just as in the stomach, the internal lining of the bladder forms into folds called *rugae* (ROO-jee). As urine trickles into the bladder, these rugae stretch out, allowing the bladder to swell from the size of a walnut up to the size of a grapefruit.

After about 10 ounces of urine have been collected, the pressure in the bladder increases. Nerves in the bladder send a message of fullness to the spinal cord and brain, urging you to urinate. It is possible (but not recommended) for a person to hold as much as 20 to 27 ounces of urine in his or her bladder at one time.

During toilet training, two sphincters in the bladder neck are taught to hold and release urine, just as the anal sphincter is taught to hold and release feces.

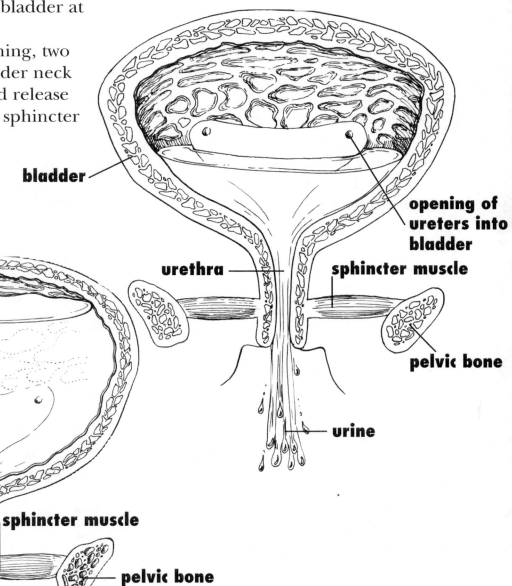

bladder

opening of ureters into bladder

urethra

sphincter muscle

pelvic bone

urine

a lot of urine

bladder

opening of ureters into bladder

urethra

sphincter muscle

pelvic bone

URETHRA

The *urethra* (you-REE-thruh) drains urine from the bladder out of the body. Like a ureter, the urethra is a muscular tube lined with mucus.

Because it runs the length of the penis, the urethra in a man measures about 8 inches. In a woman, the urethra is about 1½ inches long.

A woman's urethra and anus are located very close to each other, putting females at higher risk for urinary tract infections. By wiping from back to front with toilet paper, a woman can drag bacteria-filled feces from her anus up into her urethra.

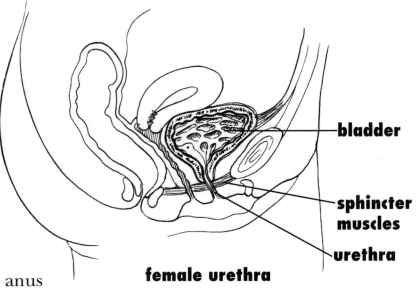

bladder

sphincter muscles

urethra

female urethra

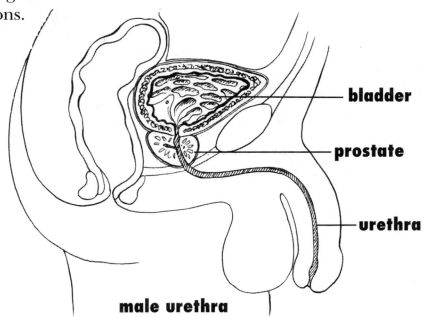

bladder

prostate

urethra

male urethra

THE SMELL IS IN THE PEE

Normal urine contains water, salts, acids, and urea. In the presence of infection or disease, urine may contain such substances as blood, crystals, protein, mucus, bacteria, or pus. Diet and environment can also change urine. For instance, the amino acids in asparagus are so small they travel through the kidneys and into the urine. This is what causes the odd smell after you've eaten this green vegetable.